Dear Mary,
all your dear ones enjoy
many of *life's blessings*
Ronnie / Verona

A Tardiness in Nature

Is it but this? A tardiness in nature
Which often leaves the history unspoke
That it intends to do.

(France's words in King Lear, Act I, ll.235-7)

Verona Anne VanderVen

A Tardiness in Nature

Copyright © 2019 by Verona Anne VanderVen

Published by Winters Publishing
www.winterspublishing.com
812-663-4948

Printed in the United States of America

ISBN: 978-1-883651-97-8

Table of Contents

Cast of Characters

Carrie - Leading Character: Wife of Matt and mother to Anna, Durinda, and Tim

Matt - Carrie's husband and father of Anna, Durinda, and Tim

Adam and Anna - Parents of Anton and grandparents of Carrie

Anton - Carrie's father

Maria I - Carrie's mother and first wife to Anton

Maria II - Carrie's stepmother and second wife to Anton

Maria III - Carrie's Aunt Mary and younger sister of Anton

Jan - Husband of Maria III and uncle to Carrie, father of Carrie's cousin

Jan - Son of Adam and Anna, brother to Maria III, Anton, and young Adam

Adam and Eve - Uncle and aunt to Carrie. Adam is brother of Anton. They are godparents to Carrie and parents of Lynn, Ed, and Lena

Betka - Sister to Carrie and Milka, and half-sister to Ria

Milka - Sister to Carrie and Betka, and half-sister to Ria

Grandma and Grandpa Fisher - Carrie's great-aunt and great-uncle; aunt and uncle to Maria I

Durinda Hansen - Carrie's high school teacher whose influence was strong

Pastor B - Carrie's confirmation pastor and mentor

Doctor Munson - Carrie's physician after Timmy's birth and mentor to Carrie

Other important characters are included in Chapter X :: The Saints in Carrie's Life

Chapter I
In The Beginning

Carrie felt the pain. It was deep. And here she was, on the expressway in the center of town, en route to pick up Matt at the park where he was doing summer work with the kids. How much of a chance should she take? Wasn't it just another mile, or a little over? It was more than nine years since Timmy was born. Then it was just one big pain and within forty-five minutes, it was all over with. Whew!

Fearful, she decided on quick action. Leaving the expressway, she turned into the downtown exit, continued on the main street, and pulled up at the back door of the police station. The officer at the door was enjoying a quiet smoke until Carrie made her announcement.

"I'm going to have a baby, and I've just had a rather deep pain. Do you think someone can drive me to the park where my husband is so he can take me to the hospital?"

The officer called to the sergeant on duty who immediately appeared. Answering her second plea, his plan differed.

"Lady, I will not be responsible for any baby being born in Westside Park. Let's get you to the hospital and we'll send someone to pick up your husband and he can drive your car. Park it right there," he pointed to the side of the building and ordered, "Phil, help her into the ambulance."

Off they rode, Carrie, the driver accompanied by another officer, racing with siren blasting down the road paved upon an old Indian trail of a century before. Their destination was the hospital named for the old lumber magnate who was not only one of the city's founders but the benevolent donator of the land upon which the hospital had been built.

Carrie was met at the emergency station with an orderly readied with a wheelchair.

"Oh, no, I can walk," she declared.

"Sorry, ma'am, I must follow orders," and the officer gently guided her into the seat. The grimace on his face revealed the relief he felt that this woman was now being taken over by someone else.

Men are fearful of pregnant ladies, particularly ones ready to deliver, Carrie realized. Emergency wasted no time assigning her to the maternity ward. A nurse greeted her and helped her get changed into the unglamorous johnny coat designed for easy access to the bod, and directed her to the bed. Unlike previous deliveries, Carrie was informed they did not prep you, as was the custom of the '50s.

Struck by the anxiety of Carrie's arrival, the emergency ward intake clerk did not proceed with normal admittance forms. When the phone rang in Carrie's room, Ginny VanderClout, the floor director who had entered to greet Carrie, answered it. Ginny knew Carrie. She was the instructor who taught the prenatal class Carrie had attended during this, her fourth pregnancy. Carrie was probably the oldest of her pregnant colleagues and astounded by the changes in preparation for delivery, over previous times. Her oldest, Anna, was now almost fifteen. How much more open these younger women were, sharing their prenatal experiences. Even sex was a much more open topic! Ginny had been a classmate of Jane, Carrie's sister-in-law, during their nurses' training many years before. Being acquainted with both Jane and Carrie, Ginny answered the questions posed by the emergency desk clerk assertively. "Well, she *does* have a registration with the hospital!" Hanging up, Ginny explained to Carrie: "You came in a police ambulance so the girl downstairs insisted that 'those kinds of people don't have a registration,' but I set her straight!"

Shortly after, Dr. Prompt entered. Puzzled by Carrie's abrupt entry, he asked, "Why didn't you call my office?" He appeared angry and frustrated. Carrie had just visited his office on the previous afternoon. Her checkup evoked his prediction, "About five or six days yet. Maybe like a fire
cracker." The Fourth was still six days away.

Carrie tried to explain. She was not near a telephone. It was not yet the day of cell phones. Her last pregnancy had ended so abruptly that the memory left her with apprehension.

'Please don't send me home," she begged.

"Well, let's see what we've got here." A hasty examination revealed two centimeters' dilation. Labor appeared to be definite.

"Let's give you a shot, that'll help you along," his voice was now more consoling.

After he left, Carrie, uncertain, almost tearful, voiced her concerns to Ginny, "My doctor's mad at me. I think he feels I shouldn't have come here the way I did."

"Never you mind, Carrie. You did the right thing. Just last week we had one baby born in a car, right here in the hospital parking lot. Don't always know how these things are going to go. Besides, honey, he's a man, even though he's a doctor. And men don't have babies. So what do they know?"

Her tone was reassuring to Carrie, who all her life had doubted herself.

Another nurse entered. It was suppertime.

"You may only order something light, nothing heavy, for you're in labor," she reminded her.

Carrie recalled how before leaving home, she had carefully set the table. Supper was prepared and ready to serve. All she had to do was go pick up Matt and the two younger children who were at the movies, and then they would all eat together. Anna, her oldest, offered to ride with her.

"No, I'll be okay, it's only about twenty minutes. Just keep the food warm."

"How about some sherbet or maybe yogurt?" the nurse's words interrupted Carrie's thoughts of home, which now seemed terribly far away.

When moments later, the sherbet was served, Carrie downed it and then settled back on the pillows propped behind her. The pains seemed to increase, but then moments later, they stopped. She tried to read. Reading, which had always been an escape mechanism ever since elementary school, now seemed to elude her. She had not yet recovered from the emotional reaction to this situation she was in, or the fear which had overtaken her when she felt the earlier pain while driving on the expressway.

Hers was the only bed in this room. She was alone, accompanied only by the stillness, which took place after all the dinner trays had been collected, carts removed, and the hallway became quiet, ushering in the evening hours.

****

Stillness, a sort of quiet void, had been a companion to Carrie for most of her life. Fear had been another. Sometimes there was guilt. Why? Away from everyone close to her now, she had time to ponder. Folks claimed a two-year-old was too young to remember. But Carrie did remember. How could she ever forget? The stillness came, but not until after the funeral was over. Maybe it was the day after. Carrie recalled awakening, and finding her father in the dining room, she listened to his reassurances. Anton put down the prayer book, or was it Tranovsky's hymnbook he was reading? He crossed the room and lifted Carrie high into the air. In response to her inquiry, he spoke in his native language, assuring Carrie she would see her mother again, *na sudny dyen*. Carrie was already bilingual enough to understand what he said: on the Judgment Day. But she did not understand what he meant. When was that day?

All Carrie could recall was seeing her mother lying there in the casket in their living room. Flowers surrounded her. Carrie called to *Tata*, as she addressed her father, that her mother needed her medicine. Why didn't someone get her medicine so she could wake up and walk?

Now the casket and the flowers were all gone. There was just her: *Tata* and Carrie. Her sisters were not there. Carrie did not even remember when they were there. Other than the vision of her mother lying in the casket, she had a vivid memory of her mother when she was still alive. They were sitting together in the family pew at their church. It was perhaps a short time, maybe two months or so before the youngest baby was born. Maria, her mother, gave Carrie a coin, probably a penny, to place in the offering plate. A penny was a lot of money in 1933. It could buy a whole bag of popcorn or a variety of wrapped candies at the confectionery store. Depression days, these were.

What Carrie was later to realize was that when she lost her mother, she also lost her siblings for a time. Betka, the fourteen-month-old, was taken into the home of her godparents. The gentle Slovak folk who articulated the vows of responsibility and guardianship at the time of the child's baptism took their commitment very seriously. Besides, they had no children of their own, and Betka was a delightful companion in their home. Mildred, the week-old baby who was delivered during Maria's final illness was kept in the home of Anton's parents. When in desperation Anton declared he would adopt her out, old Anna rejected the idea. This child was her own flesh and blood. She would raise this infant granddaughter, herself.

The happiest memories were of those many weeks spent with the great-aunt and great-uncle who lived in the southwest suburb. Carrie called them Grandma and Grandpa. Grandpa was a younger brother of Carrie's European grandmother, the mother of Carrie's mother. So his six children were first cousins to Carrie's mother. It was this man who had sponsored Carrie's mother when she left her home and family in Europe to immigrate to America, the promised land which was to fulfill the hopes and dreams of many of her contemporaries during the first quarter of the 20th century. The older cousins were already grown. The youngest son was a senior in the high school close by. All took part in caring for and entertaining Carrie, but the one who was closest to her, other than Grandma. was the oldest daughter, Anna. Carrie was to remember the warmth of their kitchen, the closeness and caring she received from their family, throughout her life.

****

"How are you doing?" the floor nurse unwittingly interrupted Carrie's reverie as she entered the room. "Are you timing your pains?" She took her temperature, felt for her pulse, and then announced, "We're going to give you a shot to help things along."

Carrie asked what was in the shot. Oxytocin. "Oh, no!" she protested. Just that morning she had been reading an article in one of the women's magazines and the author vividly described the negative effects experienced by babies whose mothers had been administered oxytocin during labor. Memories of her son Timmy's difficulties loomed in her mind.

"Doctor's orders. I'm sure he wouldn't order anything that would be harmful to you or your baby," the nurse spoke reassuringly, so Carrie held out her arm.

"Are you hungry? If so, we can get you more sherbet," the nurse offered.

Just then Matt walked in. "How are you doing?" He leaned over and pecked her cheek.

I'll leave you two alone," the nurse offered. "Ring if you need anything," and pointing to Carrie, she predicted, "Looks like you'll be here a while yet."

The crease on Matt's forehead indicated his concern. "If that's true, how come you're here now, so soon?":

After Carrie explained all that had happened, Matt related his experience.

"I sure was surprised when the officers approached me at the park." Matt explained how the contacts were made, confirmed picking up the younger daughter Durinda and Timmy at the movies. Anna had everything ready to serve, and all was under control. Almost fifteen, Anna was reliable, emulating much of Carrie's personal training. She was left in charge, freeing Matt to be with Carrie at the hospital.

"One for each of you," the nurse entered with a cup of sherbet for Matt as well as for Carrie. "Enjoy!"

"I think I could go for more, but they've restricted me to liquids for now."

This was another contrast Carrie and Matt were experiencing from their previous children's births. Husbands were not allowed to accompany their wives in the labor room. Carrie found herself mentally recounting those occasions.

****

A decade and a half ago Matt was ordered to wait in the husbands' lounge. Carrie was comforted and encouraged by an elderly nurse who massaged her back and arms, soothing her, "I know, my dear, it's been long ago, but I still remember."

Anna, their first-born, arrived at 9 a.m. but it was noon when they placed her in Carrie's arms. Motherhood gave her a sense of wholeness, completion, which she felt for the first time in her life. Previously she considered her wedding day as the happiest day in her life, but now, that first happiness was surpassed. She told this tiny child with her tiny hand curled around Carrie's little finger how much she loved her, and how she and Daddy had waited for her.

What a contrast to the birth of the second daughter! Labor for Durinda began with the thunder and lightning of an early summer thunderstorm, adding to the stressful period of Carrie's pregnancy. Matt had changed employment, exchanging the steady weekly salary insulating asbestos for a sales rep position which paid by straight commission.

Hard-sell, they called it. Supervisors held up as their champion writers like Frank Bettger, Napoleon Hill, or John M. Wilson, who shared their sales expertise with the young men setting out to make their fortunes in America's post-World War II years. Added to these were the clergy, like Norman Vincent Peale with his powers of positive thinking, or Claude M. Bristol's magic of believing. And Matt had exchanged his blue collar for that of the business suit and tie with the other young men, a goal he had expressed to Carrie one Sunday years before, after returning from worship service. Dressed in the suit he bought to wear at their wedding, he declared, "This is the way I want to dress for my job, every day."

The rain fell in torrents. After phoning his father to bring Matt's younger sister to stay with Anna, who was not quite two, Matt drove Carrie to the hospital. It was past midnight. Carrie's pains were intense, and when the young nurse examined her in the labor room she frantically announced to her patient, "Lady, you're going to have a baby in a half hour!" Leaving Carrie alone, she ran to summon the resident, who was asleep.

Disheveled and bleary eyed, the resident inquired, "When did you begin your pains?"

"About two hours ago," Carrie explained. "I waited to make sure this was the real thing."

"You sure as hell did!" and throwing down his rubber glove, he ordered, "Get this woman into the delivery room!"

A short time later Carrie's own physician arrived. His examination proved contrary.

"There's no emergency here, we have some time yet."

Carrie tearfully told him, "The other doctor is mad at me because I didn't come sooner."

The look he gave the nurse, both quizzical and disapproving, led to her defense of the resident. "It's my fault, doctor, I made a mistake when she first came in."

Subsequently, Carrie was transferred back to the labor room. There was no friendly nurse to soothe or encourage. Carrie recalled the tales of childbirth experiences told by her grandmother whose children were born in the first decade of the 20th century. Out of nine, only four lived. Added to that was the mystery of the death of her mother, a week after the birth of Milka, her youngest sister.

When the infant arrived a few hours later, Carrie cried. "Another girl?" She had hoped for a boy and had picked out a name: Timothy.

"Next time," the doctor said. Matt consoled her, "She's so cute honey, you're gonna love her anyway."

"Two girls are nice. They're company for each other." One of her ward mates had hoped for a girl and had a boy.

Anna was five and Durinda three when Carrie was expecting Timothy. What neither Carrie nor Matt could predict were the many changes that would take place in their lives with the addition of Timmy in their young family.

****

After finishing their sherbet, Carrie lay down, and Matt, poised in the chair beside her bed, opened his physics notebook. This last course would earn him his bachelor's degree. It was summer classes in the mornings, and working for the rec department afternoons, and then cramming for this last course in the evenings. While he studied, Carrie tried to relax. It was comforting to have Matt here for a few hours.

"Time for a shot," the nurse indicated that Matt could remain. "We have to help this baby along."

Three hours had passed since the first shot. Carrie wondered, would this harm the baby? She kept recalling the article in the woman's magazine, which revealed the negative possibilities for the baby whose mother was given oxytocin during labor. One was an increase in respiratory infections. Yet she also wanted to have it all over with. Not much progress in the labor since she arrived at the hospital almost four hours ago.

Then there was the fear, which continued to creep into her mind. Why? Carrie kept hearing the words of her paternal grandmother. Childbirth was a scary time in the old country. The village midwife was there to assist. Fortunate was the mother who survived. Even more fortunate, the family blessed with a live baby.

Carrie's mother had become ill during childbirth. Death took her eight days later. Family rumors told of the delivery at home. Visiting nurses and doctors came, but the illness worsened. Toxemia? Childbed fever? It was the early thirties, long before the discovery of penicillin and the medical marvels that could save a mother from becoming a fatality. In the final days, she was removed to the hospital. Carrie wondered, if something should happen to me, what would become of my children?

Carrie faced the harsh reality of her absent mother when Anna was born. Her roommate and the other moms at the hospital all had mothers to visit them with promises of visits and arrangements for help when they arrived home. Now the void became prominent in Carrie's mind.

When she was young, people at her church talked about God and told her, her mother was with Him. Why would God take away her mother when she was so needed here? When she was expecting Timmy, no matter how tired she felt, she would read to the girls every night before bedtime. They covered the whole series of Laura Ingalls' books and laughingly pretended that the girls were Mary and Laura. Carrie wanted them to remember her and the care she gave them at this time.

Although most of the new mothers were to remain at the hospital for a week, Carrie longed to go home. She begged the doctor to release her and Anna on the fourth day. She wanted to be with Matt. When the doctor asked who would be helping her, she lied, "My grandmother is coming."

Tears fell on the seventh day, her third day home. Carrie was nursing Anna, caring for her completely. She was in love with this child. So was Matt. Yet, somehow they missed communications completely. Matt had to work. Housework and dishes piled up. Lacking a washing machine and living in the days before the advent of disposable diapers, Matt did valiantly wash all cloth diapers by hand. No one had briefed the husband on the necessity for rest for the new mother. He was annoyed at Carrie's weeping.

"How could you be sad when we have such a beautiful baby?" he chided her and lifting up the week-old Anna, he promised her, "Don't worry, Daddy will take care of you."

Matt's mother lived ten miles away, but Carrie did not call her for help. The relationship had been strained ever since Matt and Carrie were asked to move away from the apartment they were renting behind the folks' store. Was this a generational conflict? There were unmet expectations from both sides. Carrie recalled how one author claimed that people from another generation were really from another race. (*Dandelion Wine*) The older couple asked Matt to pay rent. They also expected him to mind the store a number of hours each day. His job called for swing shift hours, 3 to 11 p.m. Carrie worked as a clerk-receptionist during the months before her pregnancy brought about her resignation, sometime during her fifth month. They hoped she would fill in the remaining hours of the day, but Matt forbade her to do so unless the folks agreed to waive rent payments. Actually, what he was possibly manifesting was a pent-up emotional storm which had been evolving since his own childhood. When Matt's father presented them with a written request to move, Carrie phoned her Aunt Mary, Maria III, as she categorized her mentally, to separate the Marias who had influenced her life.

She had made her home with Maria III during her teen years. Aside from attending high school, she worked part-time after school. During those years she held 17 jobs altogether. It was World War II during which time it was easy to get part-time employment. What she did not know was that when she very resentfully handed over her paychecks to Maria III, the aunt had placed much of her money into a savings account, doling out just enough for bus fare to school and a mite for spending money. Lunch came in a paper bag.

After Carrie married Matt and learned of these savings, she had called Jan, the husband of Maria III, with the hope that she and Matt could purchase a car. Jan jokingly refused. His reasons? They could not afford to maintain a car on their income. It was not just the gas, he explained. There were oil changes, tires, brakes to be fixed, and other repairs. Carrie retorted, "What can I do when I'm in labor, how will I get to the hospital?"

"Don't you have friends who can take you?"

Now Carrie had a new request. Answering an ad in the Sunday paper, she and Matt went to look at a bungalow advertised for sale. The owner greeted them warmly. She was even agreeable to lowering the down payment, just the right amount that Maria III had saved for Carrie. This time Maria and Jan found the request to be appropriate. A home? Yes. How much for the monthly payment? The interest? Lowered from 6% to 5%, paid on a land contract directly to the owner. The aunt sent a bank draft for the deposit, and the next month Matt, with the help of friends, moved their furnishings into the little bungalow. Matt's father drove up just as the last load was placed in the truck, and surprised, he spoke to the wife of the truck driver, "I think this is for the best. They need to be out on their own."

The grandparents were happy though, when Anna was born, and lavished Carrie with flowers and a mini bouquet set in a tiny pitcher for the baby. Matt's father greeted Carrie warmly and his mother kissed Carrie's cheek. They were delighted to have a grandchild. Later, they left a number of baby clothes Matt's mother had saved from his babyhood in a wrapped package between the screen door and locked front door. Matt was still fuming from their disagreement and returned the package with a note telling them that he now lived on the north end and they were on the south end, where he wished they would remain.

Months later, when Anna was six months old, Carrie's mother-in-law ventured to their home. It was late afternoon and Matt was away at work. Carrie proudly bathed little Anna, fed her, and let her paternal grandmother hold her while she prepared them some dinner. The older woman asked Carrie's forgiveness earlier upon telephoning to see how the baby was doing. Carrie calmly told her own feelings of being rejected and deprived of a home with the forthcoming baby. Her mother-in-law seemed very sincere in seeking reconciliation.

Was it the words of Grandma Anna on her wedding day that Carrie now recalled, charging her to respect Matt's mother as her own new mother, or was it the sincerity in the voice of her mother-in-law which lured her into a reconciliation? Whatever their drawbacks, Carrie knew that Matt's parents were strong Christian believers. Their faith was based on the literal words of Scripture, which they read faithfully each day. Prayers were spoken at every meal. Church attendance was twice a Sunday, sometimes three.

Carrie pondered on her own faith. What did she believe and why? Was it Solzhenitsyn's character who declared when it thunders and lightnings, try *not* believing? Well, she could easily paraphrase him now, for when labor pains begin, try not believing!

****

Religion. Where did it begin and where would it end? For Carrie it began when her father spoke of the Judgment Day, the day when she would see her mother again. But he couldn't tell her when that day would be.

After Anton had been remarried for a year, and Carrie had begun first grade at the public school, the decision was made that Carrie would also attend church school. Slovak School, they called it. On Saturday mornings Anton would walk with Carrie the three short blocks to Chicago Avenue where Carrie boarded the streetcar that was to take her to the corner of Springfield Avenue. From there it was one long block to walk to the church.

Classes were held below the Sanctuary, in the church basement. Attending were children of all ages from six to fourteen. Luther's Catechism and certain Bible stories were taught in the native tongue during those earliest years. A mixture of Czech and Slovak, or a Czechified Slovak as some would call it. Scripture was taught from the *Kralice* Bible, which had been translated during the time of Wycliffe, when the Bohemian princess had become queen of

England. In order to facilitate learning about their faith in the native language, the students studied the language as well.

Anton was determined to help Carrie. "A, a, a, b, c, c," she repeated the letters of the alphabet. They sounded like *ah, beh, tse.* Prime memory years took hold and provided Carrie a familiarity with the language for all of her life. There are actually fourteen variations of the Slavic languages. Often it was possible for Carrie to understand immigrants from Poland or Croatia, the Ukraine or other Slavic countries, when hearing them speak on the streetcar or in stores where the family shopped.

It was the religion that took a long time for Carrie to regard seriously. Carrie considered why. Maybe there were two reasons. One resulted from Maria II's influence upon Anton. Believing that the amount of religious training at the church school was inadequate, she convinced Anton that his three daughters must be taught more at home. Just as her strict clergyman uncle had required of her, Maria demanded that the three must memorize numerous pages of Biblical History in the native language. Weekly assignments were given to each. Usually Saturday afternoon was recitation time. Failure to memorize and recite the given assignment was followed by punishment, the leather strap or a wooden ruler.

Carrie recalled how on one Saturday morning Betka confided to her that she could not remember all of her assignment. Carrie made her a tiny crib sheet with the words carefully written. It could be held inside the palm of Betka's hand, and Carrie told her to stand directly to the side of and about a step back behind Anton, whose eyes would be on the contents of the book as she recited. Unfortunately, Maria II entered the room and caught the little girl attempting to read the words aloud. The punishment Betka received haunted Carrie with guilt for many years.

In the beginning years of church school, Carrie and the other children were taught by the pastor of the church. Then for a very short time there was an interim teacher named Mr. Socha. He taught the grammar in such an interesting way that Carrie felt very comfortable at the school. He also taught the children a Slovak folk song which Carrie remembered all of her life. This teacher's tenure was short-lived, however. The church council then hired a man who was also a public school teacher and principal.

Mr. Nemudry, as Carrie came to call him, was very biased against the Roman Catholic Church. He spent many hours during the forthcoming years blasting away at and deriding the Catholics. He expounded on all the old Reformation era sins. Very little was taught about the love of Jesus, the gospels, or the history of the Hebrews as recorded in the Old Testament. These Carrie and her sisters learned about from the memorization required at home. She remembered sharing the story of Moses leading the Israelites out of Egypt with the painter who had come to paint her Grandma's home in the suburbs during her visit there one summer. The painter expressed surprise at Carrie's knowledge and commended her for it.

Besides the avid denunciations of the Catholics, Nemudry's pedagogy left much to be desired. Carrie, who absorbed all that he had stated, would sometimes repeat his claims to classmates in the public school. These produced fights, for most of her classmates were members of the large Catholic Church in the neighborhood. It behooves adults to be more conscientious of how they influence young children.

Possibly the only creditable memory Carrie could recall of Nemudry was that he had a great interest in music, and that he wanted to have the students perform commendably during church services, as required. One particular hymn, which was sung at the installation service of the pastor who would later be her confirmation and first communion celebrant, was sung to the tune of Sibelius's *Finlandia.* Often, even in adulthood, Carrie found herself repeating the words before falling asleep:

> Be still my soul, the Lord is on thy side
> Bear patiently the cross of grief or pain;
> Leave to thy God to order and provide;
> In ev'ry change He faithful will remain.
> Be still, my soul; thy best, thy heavenly Friend
> Through thorny ways leads to a joyful end.

That was as close as Carrie could come to a relationship with God for many years. When religious training is not accompanied with love—God's love—it means nothing. Less than nothing. It turns the recipient away from the harsh treatment and leaves unhappy memories.

Yet Carrie did recall many people who had shown her kindness in her young life. Only recently, during this past year when she expressed her fear to Dr. Mudry when anticipating the first test in the college course in Russian, she found him to be reassuring. Was she fearful of failure or was she fearful that she would not measure up? Were those fears of punishment from childhood still haunting her?

Dr. Mudry reminded her that Satan tries to cultivate fear within us. "Remember how Martin Luther picked up an inkwell and threw it at the Devil?"

The year before, she was enrolled in an education course at the college in Grand Rapids. The class met at 4 p.m., less than an hour after Carrie's fourth-graders were dismissed. There were thirty-six in all, and Carrie was determined that this, her first year of teaching, would be a success. She was determined also to reach every student. She wrote essays about her classroom experiences, observations of her students, activities she planned. In spite of her excitement at teaching, she flunked the first test. Her points were too low. When she approached the instructor, he proved to be surprisingly understanding. Giving her an alternate assignment, he commended her on her enthusiasm for teaching.

Later, when commenting on her writing, he spoke not with pity, but with a conviction of fact: "I can tell someone has hurt this person."

Carrie wondered, how had this man gained this insight? Faith? Wasn't it Aquinas who taught that faith would produce understanding? This certainly refuted those who believed that understanding would produce faith.

It has been reported that often when a person is drowning, his whole life unfolds before him. Carrie wondered, is this why she was now reminiscing? Memories that had been buried in her subconscious for years were now being resurrected. Were Grandma Anna's old fears of childbirth attempting to take hold? Or did she, like Luther, need an inkwell to throw at the Devil?

Chapter II
Adam and Anna

Adam was the first to arrive to the "promised land." Anna followed him just two years later.

Who were Adam and Anna? Carrie recalled Adam, her father's father, as being a quiet man. After he had retired from the railroad, his day was spent looking for usable refuse in neighbors' yards, peeking in refuse barrels with the intent to collect enough scrap metal to trade it with the itinerant peddler who came by bi-weekly in his horse drawn wagon. Traveling in the alley behind the homes, he would call aloud, "Rags and iron!"

The coins in exchange for the metal, tin cans, leather, or anything of value would provide Adam with the tobacco for his pipe. Carrie remembered how sweet was the odor from his pipe's contents. The pipe and the nocturnal *medetsinka*—actually a small glass of whiskey at bedtime—were Adam's only indulgences. Anna did cook his favorite meals, recipes she was taught to prepare in their native village. There were home-cooked soups, *polievka* with *rezance,* homemade egg noodles. Poppy seed *kolach* or loaves filled with crushed walnuts. Carrie's favorite were those with *lekvar,* loaves or tarts filled with delicious prune jelly.

Recalling her grandfather, Carrie realized she had not built a relationship with the old man. Yet now she looked back on her memory of him with fondness, especially realizing the foundation of faith he had offered. It was on little Milka's first birthday. The evening darkness of early March was lit by only one small candle on the young sister's birthday cake. Adam, hands folded and head bowed in reverence, offered a prayer of thanksgiving for this first year of Milka's life. Standing centered around the table was the entire family: Anton, his younger sister Maria, with her husband Jan, their daughter Ann, Carrie, young Adam with his wife, Eve, and their children, and the matriarch, Anna, who was to cut the cake and serve the awaited dessert. Carrie liked it when the family was all-together like this.

Looking back on those early years, Carrie remembered the absence of any emotion toward old Adam. There was neither love nor hatred. Rather, one might consider her feelings to be neutral, as they were toward many adults, except for those she felt toward her father. Sometimes she remembered eating the leftover sandwich from Adam's lunch. Always hungry, she did not even mind the soggy bread and lettuce tucked around the lunchmeat remaining in Adam's lunch pail when he returned home from his day at the railroad yards.

One incident occurred after Anton had been married to Maria II for several years and all his children had been united with him. There was boisterous action in their apartment which was situated above the basement where Adam had his tools and collected items. Climbing up the narrow steps, he approached the apartment with complaints about the noise. When Carrie explained that it was *Milka* that was running around, old Adam defended her, believing she was too small for her feet to make that much noise. Carrie boldly told him that Milka could make noise like a *slon*, an elephant.

This retort brought a chuckle from Maria II.

Another incident occurred when Carrie was a junior in high school. Her teacher of American Lit asked the students to find out from their parents and grandparents the reasons why they came to America. Prompted by her English teacher, Carrie approached Adam, who was now well past seventy years old, and questioned him. Why did you leave your homeland? He answered plainly, "*Nemaly sme chleb.*"

"We had no bread." It would be many years later that Carrie would learn of Adam's decision to leave the land in his home village to seek not his fortune, but a decent livelihood in America. It was the turn of the century and American corporations were hiring immigrants for less wages than seasoned Americans were willing to be paid. Adam left Anna with his sons and year-old daughter Maria (later the Maria III to Carrie). What he really left behind was the pastoral village for the bustling busy city of Chicago at the beginning of the twentieth century.

A later generation would relish this same village as a desirable weekend get-away. Here families would gather, not only to escape the busy workaday town life, but also utilize the land the family owned to grow a large percentage of their food. Vegetables such as beets, potatoes, peppers, leaf lettuce, chard, cabbage, tomatoes, and berry bushes, apple and pear trees—all would serve, canned and frozen, as valued supplements to the family's food supply. Chickens, lambs, and a cow, as well as a flock of geese, provided protein. These necessities enabled them to survive on meager monetary wages. Doctors and teachers earned in one month what their American counterparts brought home after about two days' wages.

During the Cold War of the fifties, Carrie recalled it was Anna who later commended her husband for removing his family from the poverty and politics that now prevailed. She explained to Carrie how grateful she was that Adam had chosen to leave their native land.

Yet this transfer had not been without sorrow. For after Adam had been in Chicago for two years, he sent for Anna. She took Maria, now three years old, with her, but had to leave the boys behind.

Aged ten and twelve, the young Adam and Anton remained with relatives in the village. The intent was to return for the boys on the following year. But their plan was interrupted by the assassination in Sarajevo. The boys grew to be young men before they joined their parents in America, in the early 1920s.

Carrie remembered Anton telling Maria III when both brother and sister were beyond middle age and bidding each other "S *Bohom*"— good-bye (literally "Go with God"), that when as a youngster in the village he had kissed her and bid her goodbye, he feared he would never see her again. Maria recalled how her mother often expressed tearful concern for her two sons who were far away, and enduring the hardships of World War I.

Anna was ten years younger than Adam. The family tale which Carrie remembered was that after Anna's mother had died and her father's new wife had proven to be difficult to live with, she left her father's home. A native Slovak friend once explained to Carrie that a custom accepted by many villages was that the stepmother as the new mistress of the home often evaded all responsibility for her predecessor's children by evicting them from their father's home. Orphaned, these children often became vulnerable to the dregs of society. They were exploited by employers who paid meager wages. When Adam met Anna, his love and also perhaps his pity for the young woman led him to invite her to live with him. She accepted and six months later, they were married.

Anna gave birth to nine children, of which four survived. Anton, born in 1901, was the first to live. Adam, whom Anna named after her husband, was born two and a half years later. Maria, the only daughter, was born in 1910. Jan, the youngest son, was born after Anna joined Adam in America.

Adam and Anna shared their home with other newcomers to America. Most of them were temporary boarders who were living on their meager incomes with intent to save enough money to bring other family members to America. Their mainstay was their Slovak community and church. Yet their allegiance to their new land was wholeheartedly expressed. Carrie wondered, years later, why Anna did not have the foresight to encourage her children to study and acquire a higher education. No one provided her with this guidance. They were only accustomed to physical labor.

Anton and Adam both had difficulties with employment in areas of their interest. There were language barriers for them as well. Adam expressed greater independence than Anton by leaving the family home and going out on his own. He met the love of his life, Eve. It was Eve who became Carrie's godmother. Carrie counted her as one of the saints in her young life. She felt a kinship with this woman who seemed to understand her.

Yet Eve was open and honest with Carrie when correction was required. Carrie, never feeling she belonged to either segments of the family, was living on her own when she had finished high school. Working in downtown Chicago, she stayed away, but occasionally phoned her Aunt Eve. Added to Carrie's confusion was the society to which she was now exposed. It was an adult world where many adults were acting like children. She was not sure what her relationship with Matt would be in the future. She discussed this somewhat with her aunt. Yet when her aunt suggested Carrie come to visit so they could talk things over, the visit never took place. The suburb was some distance away and going by train was not easily arranged for Carrie who was working at two different jobs to make ends meet. Only seventeen, she was attempting to support herself independently.

Aunt Eve's daughter, Lynn, phoned to tell Carrie that Grandpa Adam had died. His body lay in state. Carrie did not go to the funeral home or to the funeral. She did not want to see the rest of the family from whom she felt distant, unloved and rejected. Later, Eve admonished her: "It would have been only right for you to go and pay your last respect to your grandfather."

She explained that Carrie could at least have visited the funeral home during early afternoon hours when few viewers of the body would be present.

Anna continued to live alone after Adam's death. Her spoken English was limited, although in her many years in the country she did learn to understand much of what others were saying. The village ways of sizing up situations had never left her. Childbirth was a condition to be feared. Money was to be saved and invested in order to make more money. Once or twice she was victimized by investments, which resulted in losses. Yet some of her savings were responsible for the success of one budding business, which ultimately expanded into a popular clothing store patronized by the Slovak community. Weddings, graduations, Easter outfits, and other special occasions led many of the immigrants to the store. It was not until many years later that Betka learned of the start this clothier had gotten from loans provided to him by their grandmother.

What other immigrants were aware of, that Anna missed completely, was the opportunity for education of her children. Maria II and Jan, the youngest son, did complete an eighth grade education. Both had attended the elementary school located just two blocks away from their home. Anton and Adam were deprived of both the American language instruction and the social contacts which the Chicago public schools offered. They arrived as young men, with only a meager background of what the village had offered them, and lacked the tools needed to succeed in the urban environment in which they had been thrust. Anna required that the earnings from their physical labor be paid to her each payday. Anton dutifully remained with his parents, happily obliging his mother for the years prior to his marriage to Maria.

Adam, however, rebelled against this type of arrangement. He moved out of their home and went to live on his own, preferring to pay room and board elsewhere. When he met Eve, he fell madly in love with the beautiful lady. Their affair led to marriage and the birth of their daughter Lynn. Both had been endowed with a strong work ethic. Adam was wise enough to study some English. After working for a steel company, he applied and was accepted to a more attractive position at the large electric company which supplied Chicago with its power. Creative, Adam used his position as maintenance man to learn how to build steel items. Carrie recalled the gift of the lovely sturdy Christmas tree stand he gave to her and Matt. Adam made other decorative items such as weathervanes. One found its home on the roof of their house.

Adam and Eve had two other children, a son, Edmund and little Lena who was born after the death of Maria. All attended the church school with Carrie. There were several incidents which Carrie's cousins reported to their parents. It was obvious that Mr. Nemudry, the church schoolteacher, often verbally abused Carrie. Once Lynn's report to her father brought Adam, Carrie's godfather, into a confrontational meeting with the instructor. Adam seemed to know that Carrie was unable to complain of this treatment to her own father. Later, when the teacher was scolding Carrie for chatting with her seatmate, Nemudry addressed Lynn, complaining, "See, and then people accuse me of picking on her!"

Carrie remembered her cousin Lynn being an influence on her young life. She admired the older cousin who once, at the age of about six years, played Barber with her and trimmed Carrie's hair which brought laughter to those who observed the primitive results. They were only children at play. During adolescence, Carrie imitated much that she saw Lynn do. The older teen experimented with make-up. Seeking an identity and poise, Carrie copied her older cousin, never considering whether imitating her cousin was correct for her, personally.

Lynn Ann, as she was named, was another of the matriarch's granddaughters who carried her name. Each time a daughter, daughter-in-law, or granddaughter was expecting, old Anna insisted the girl must be named after her. There were Ann, and Carrie herself, carried Ann for a middle name. It did not end there, however. When Carrie was expecting her first child, she was again advised that if this one proved to be a girl as her grandmother already foretold, she must be named Ann. Carrie obliged her grandmother Anna. Although she named her second daughter after her most favorite teacher, Durinda, the middle name was Ann.

Grandmother Anna influenced Carrie in other ways as well. Probably the most momentous influence was on her wedding day. After Anna had met Matt's mother, she told Carrie: "See, you have now been given another mother. You must cherish her."

Anna spoke of Jeanette with authority. The young Carrie consciously or subconsciously followed this advice for many years of her married life. Perhaps recalling this admonition created some of the conflicts during those early years of her marriage to Matt.

Other childhood memories loomed in Carrie's mind. There were the repeated disagreements between Anton and his mother. After Maria II learned of the years of giving his paycheck to his parents, she continuously prodded Anton to demand some of his money from old Anna. Anna repeatedly told her children they would receive their inheritance *after she was gone*.

Post-Depression days created many hardships for Anton.

Unemployment and uncertainty of income brought him to ask Anna to agree to omit rent payments. Somehow there was enough food, but very little funds for rent or luxuries. Clothing for the three sisters often came from the charity parcels of the former employers of Maria II. Her periodic visits to these former employers meant bringing home with her clothes that their own daughters had outgrown or no longer wished to wear. Carrie remembered one particular garment that had a pattern on each side. One week she wore the dress with the printed pattern on one side. The following week, after turning the dress inside out, she wore the plain colored pattern with sleeves trimmed in the print used on the reverse side. This was a school dress for two weeks. It was only worn at school. Immediately upon returning home it was removed and hung in the closet to be ready for the following day. House clothes consisted of over-all pants and a blouse designed for play, also out of the visiting parcel. To this day, Carrie despised jeans, even though her contemporaries and even her children considered them to be "cool."

Life in the apartment located above the garage behind Adam and Anna's home only continued for Carrie until she was not quite thirteen years old.

It was very difficult for Carrie and her sisters to have a happy relationship with their grandparents. It seemed that there were continual conflicts. Some took place between Grandma Anna and Maria II. Sometimes between Maria II and Maria III. Most of the conflicts evolved from financial difficulties which Anton and Maria II were having. These were the thirties, post-Depression days.

Anton was laid off by the railroad. Unemployed, he walked the streets, looking for work, applying at every possible opportunity. He never wanted to be subjected to welfare.

Finally, an electric company right in the neighborhood offered him a job. But this meant working the swing shift. So Anton was home mornings with Maria II and little Ria, the daughter that was born to them the year following their marriage. When Carrie, Betka, and Milka arrived home from school in the afternoon, their father had already left for work. They had only Maria II. After her first year with Maria II, Carrie was now joined by her other two sisters. Grandma Anna was willing to give up Milka, now four, to allow her to join Anton's family, though at the time Anton remarried, she had declared that she intended to personally care for Milka for life. This gave Maria II an additional child to care for now. Little Ria was only a few months old.

Was it sibling rivalry that caused Maria III to sometimes criticize Maria II? Carrie recalled a memory of a visit to their apartment. Maria III brought a little undergarment for Milka, one designed with buttons to hold up the long stockings little girls wore when cold weather began in late fall.

Maria II wept after the visit, telling Anton she felt that his family did not consider her to be a fit mother. Anton tried to console her. Later he asked his sister to be more considerate.

Another time it was Anton who was confronted by Maria III. Grandma Anna wanted him to write a letter to the family in Europe. It seemed that they had received word from another family in the church that a relative had become ill. Anton was not unwilling to write the letter, but since his time was limited, he proposed doing so on the following weekend. The timing was not agreeable to Maria III. She arranged for another friend to write the letter and then vehemently accused Anton of "not even willing to write a letter for his mother, after all she has done for you."

Household tasks were not easy for Maria II. She and Anton did not own a washer. This meant that Maria II had to wash the clothing by hand. First the washtub had to be filled with hot water by hand. Then after scrubbing each item of clothing, rinsing and making certain the soap was removed, another twist before hanging the clothes on ropes outdoors. One always hoped for a sunny Monday. The alternative was to hang clothes on ropes in the basement section beneath the apartment. Sometimes clothes took two days to dry, especially in the winter. Happy was the day when Anton and Maria II were finally able to buy a wash machine. A friend told them of one that someone had for sale after replacing it with a *Spindrier*. Now the clothes could be rinsed through a wringer instead of being squeezed by hand.

Once Jan, the younger brother of Maria III who made his home with the family, suggested that the two women share their washer with Anton's wife. This was explained as being impractical as each woman has her own way of washing clothes.

Carrie wondered later, was it possible that Grandma Anna who had unhappy memories of her own stepmother, the *macocha* back in Europe, now approached Maria II with the displaced aggression she may have felt toward her own father's wife?

One cannot really understand Adam and Anna without considering the history of their people in Europe. Slovak people were always under someone. In ancient times there were the Romans. Later, the Germans. In fact, it was after one particularly loved King Charles IV whom Carrie was named: *Karolina.* Charles IV was responsible for many unique institutions in the Czech lands while he reigned over Bohemia and Germany. There was Charles University in Prague, the first secular university in Europe. The beautiful Charles Bridge in Prague overlooking the River Moldau. His achievements went far beyond those of the emperors who were ruling at the time Adam and Anna were born and living in their country in Europe.

By the time of their ascent, the Hapsburgs had become quite dysfunctional and certainly not in touch with the needs of the people within their domain. The Slovaks had adapted to the domination of the Turks for a century and a half. Even some of their Gothic church steeples had been replaced by mosque-type cupolas. Their women went about with heads covered, which Carrie and her friends were told were *babushkas,* but they survived. They learned from the Turks how to use spices; they drank the dark black inky coffee their way and even incorporated some of their language into their own. By the time of the Revolution in 1848, the unrest of many peoples within the Holy Roman Empire was being manifested. Perhaps they, like the French, led by Napoleon, also strived for liberty, equality, and fraternity. Why so long after the Magna Carta?

"A tardiness in nature," Carrie once told Matt. Why should one people condone tyranny and injustice, oppression and deprivation for many centuries before arising in protest, when another had resolved its situation centuries before?

Carrie wondered after studying Thomas Masaryk's writings, how much did Adam and Anna realize what was happening in their homeland after they had left their two sons behind? Were the sons aware of what was going on in their own country? How much information did the village of Zavada receive?

The decade following Grandfather Adam's birth had begun to

see changes in his homeland. It was an awakening. A new national consciousness was emerging. In the next three decades Masaryk, Benes and others became actively engaged in creating an awareness of human rights to the people and in attempting to present and gain these rights from the monarchy. They looked back to centuries holding a glorious past. Now during the battles of World War I, in spite of many obstacles, progress toward an independent nation was being made. Slovak soldiers earlier conscripted to fight for Austria-Hungary and imprisoned by the various Allied nations, were released to join their own Czecho-Slovak troops to fight alongside the Allies, proving their dedication and ability to return and govern their own nation.

The Czechs and Slovaks had always considered themselves brothers. At one time, together with the Polish and other Slavic peoples they shared a common empire. The Great Moravian Empire which was only in existence for less than a century had ushered in Christianity from Byzantium under the leadership of Prince Pribina in Nitra, Slovakia. The separation of the Slovaks from the Czechs took place with the Magyar invasion and eventually subjected the Slovaks to the Hungarian masters in a feudal system. This was to continue until the dissolution of the Austria-Hungary Empire in 1918. So the national awakening that had begun with the Czechs gradually but definitively spread to the Slovak people. If the sons of Adam and Anna were aware of this national awakening and its promises of improving their lot, their primary goal was to join their parents in America.

Before Anton and Adam were to leave Europe, the new country was to be rebuilding from scratch, from 1918 on. The two young brothers who had been left behind by their parents were born in Austria-Hungary but now they were teen-age residents of this new country named Czechoslovakia. War had made them hungry, cold, and deprived. Their formative years saw them growing up without the personal nurture of their parents. Nor was the social structure under which they had been born capable of nurturing or educating them to prepare for an adulthood wherein they could strive to reach their full potential, "the pursuit of happiness," as was the promise of America.

Yet America did not fulfill this promise to them. Nor did their parents lead their younger sister Maria to strive for any other method of earning her livelihood except the employment of physical labor.

Anton was to arrive first. It seemed that young Adam was delayed because of an eye problem. Carrie never learned the full details. But fortunately, Adam was to join the family about six months later. The two brothers entered their parents' home which held not only Maria III, their younger sister, and brother Jan who was born in America, but their parents were also giving shelter to two other emigrants whose room and board payments helped the family's income. The boarders were working to save enough money to provide passage for their own families to join them.

Chicago was bustling from its postwar adjustments. Corporations were ready and willing to hire workers from overseas. As yet there were no unions established to protect the employees and it was only by many personal sacrifices that this first generation to arrive survived. Often their situation and the limitations it imposed were not realized until many trials and errors were experienced. Some looked for a better future for their children and set about to arrange for it. Others, naïve and succumbing to fulfilling daily needs, saw their children as a means of added income through immediate employment. Like Anna, the matriarch, they sought to build a savings account with the money her sons had earned as an assurance of future security.

Anton followed the path that his parents led. For a number of years he worked beside his father as a carmen's helper for the railroad. How his ambitions, expressed much later, were to be thwarted were not realized for some time to come.

After Timmy's birth that was followed by her illness and recovery, Carrie was determined to learn more about her family history. She wrote Anton and his reply offered only a glimpse of her mother's family. It was later, in her college studies that Carrie delved into the history of her grandparents' homeland. 1848 and Metternich caught her deep interest, for it was after this that Magyar suppression of the Slovak people became intense. By the time the elder Adam was born in 1869 they were subjects or victims of a feudal system. The Magyars who considered themselves the dominant race sought to keep the peasants ignorant, fit only to till the soil. They also wanted to destroy the national consciousness of the Slovak people.

When Adam was still a child, in 1874 and 1875, all Slovak secondary schools maintained by private subscriptions were closed. In all State schools Magyar was the only language of instruction. By the early twentieth century Magyar teachers were even forbidden to use Slovak as a medium for teaching Magyar. It was hoped to crush out the use of the Slovak language by raising up a generation that would despise it, as "the language of ignorance." And, unfortunately, many Slovaks who were better educated became Magyar in all but origin.

Petty tyranny was enacted. One example was forbidding high school students from wearing embroidered shirts. To do so was considered an "unfriendly demonstration to the government." Of course, this caused Slovaks more than ever to preserve their national costumes and their language. Slovaks were outnumbering the Magyar population, which threatened the ruling class. Picture living in a small Slovak town before World War I. Magyar was the language of the wealthy and official classes, schools, and colleges. Some Slovaks, wanting to raise themselves in the social scale by speaking Magyar, tried to disguise their origin. Others sought to free their nation and worked quietly to this end together with the Czechs and Slovaks in other countries. When Jan Matuska wrote the words that were set to the tune of ancient melody *Nad Tatrou sa blyska* that was to become the country's national anthem, it awakened the Slovak people to claim their freedom and to band together in this endeavor. In spite of every effort against them, Slovaks continued to speak Slovak and to be Slovak in feeling.

Adam, like many Slovaks, became indignant and after becoming forty, decided to seek a new and better life in America. Adam and Anna were gone from their homeland when the Revolution on October 30, 1918 took place. The Central Slovak National Council issued a declaration at *Turčiansky Svaty Martin* (Saint Martin of Tours which Communists later shortened to the name Martin) to the effect that the Slovaks regarded themselves as an integral part of the new Czechoslovak nation and more than one hundred local Slovak National Councils identified themselves with this declaration. Many Slovaks who had previously renounced their ethnic origin under the Magyars now outwardly became Slovaks of the Slovaks. They were referred to as "Octobrists" because of their sudden change of views dated from the declaration of October 30. The sympathy of some still remained Magyar, causing a difficult element to exist in the new Republic. Jewish business people, formerly supportive of the Magyars, now showed a change of front when the language formerly despised had now become the language of the State. Their children were at once sent to Slovak teachers to be tutored.

As for Anton and young Adam, this political change did not benefit them. They had been deprived of an education that would help them to reach their full potential. Absent from their parents during the great war and its after-math, their longing for home with their parents superseded any other motive or objective in their lives. They arrived in America to join their parents, but their early deprivation was to handicap them in their lives in the new world.

Yet as Carrie pondered on their history, she realized that in spite of their uphill battle to survive in their new land, they were spared other adversities: World War II with its Nazi invasion; then the dominance of the communist regime which was to dominate the land of her parents and grandparents for many years. So old Anna was correct when she lauded her husband Adam for removing their family from their homeland.

Chapter III
Anton

It would be years and long beyond her childhood before Carrie could begin to appreciate how Maria's death must have affected Anton. Not only had he been left without his wife, but he also witnessed the changes of the whole group dynamics of his family.

His mother Anna, the matriarch of the family, had convinced him that she could care for the infant Milka. Betka, the fourteen-month-old, was being cared for by her godparents. Carrie spent some of her time with her grandmother while Anton went to work, but weekday nights and weekends he devoted to Carrie. Just two years and four months old, she was probably the only one of his children who had memories of Maria. Anton consoled her. Sometimes, by doing so, he, too, was consoled.

Only once did she remember a disciplinary action, a spanking. Carrie recalled it must have been a Saturday, for that was the day when Anton did not have to go to work and was able to attend to home chores. He prepared the windows for winter, including the one in the bedroom, which was close enough to the bed so that Carrie could reach it. The putty was still pliable and moist. The evening was warm, and Carrie reached out through the screenless open window and pressed on the substance, which was just like the clay they had in preschool, making figures and shapes. It was not until he had told several stories that Anton became aware of what Carrie was doing, while lying there on the bed, listening. Exasperated, Anton scolded and spanked. He had worked all day puttying windows, and this one would have to be done over again.

Carrie snuggled beside her father at bedtime, and after prayers were said he often sang to her, or told her stories about his native country. He related these only in the native language, and what neither father nor daughter were yet to realize was that Carrie was absorbing the Slavic tongue as well as the content of the stories and songs. Father and daughter went everywhere together.

Saturday mornings she accompanied Anton to the shoemaker's. Like a European pub, this was somewhat of a gathering place for the Slovak men to come, not just to have shoes repaired, but to exchange current news of their families, their jobs, and current events in the U.S. as well as correspondence from families in Europe. They spoke of political changes taking place. The year 1933 saw new leadership in Germany, Czechoslovakia's neighbor. Adolph Hitler had become chancellor. His propaganda denounced both democracy and the treaty of Versailles. Speculation took place. Yet no one foresaw the horrors of what was to take place in the next few years. The visitors to the cobbler's shop were proud of their kinsmen, Masaryk, Štefanik, and Beneš, whose leadership had brought about a new nation out of the ashes of old Austria-Hungary. Masaryk helped them to recall their past, back to the times when Bohemia and Germany had been ruled by Charles IV, and earlier, when the humanitarian king Wenceslaus ruled. Czechs and Slovaks both were reminded of their glorious past, long before the Thirty Years' War.

Now, under Masaryk, changes were taking place—though more in the Czech area of the country than in Slovakia. Promises and hopes ran high. Education for the young would be a priority. Anton remembered his own deprivation in boyhood. The village school was limited. He learned to read and to write and some simple mathematics. Religion was also taught in the native tongue: Bible history taught from the *Kralice* Bible and Luther's Catechism, giving just enough training in the language to give the children a reading base. The church of the Augsburg Confessions aimed to provide a spiritual and moral base. The children worked as had the generations preceding them, tasks aimed at simple agriculture and animal husbandry, construction and maintenance of their dwelling places, many built of wood from the forests surrounding them or stones gathered from the valleys and the fields. The only families whose children were able to go beyond the primary level were those who consented to have their children in Hungarian schools where the Slovak language was not recognized as an official language. After the Revolution of 1848, it had become the policy of the administration to attempt to obliterate the Slovak language completely.

Anton, with his younger brother Adam, was left in Europe, in the country that was still Austria-Hungary during World War I. Some of his memories as he described them to Carrie were very beautiful: sheep grazing in the mountainside, the village folk dancing, wearing their native costumes, and celebrating special occasions such as weddings, birthdays, and national holidays. There were also hardships of which he told Carrie and her sisters when they were together again.

During the war Anton was stricken with diphtheria. He related how difficult it was to breathe. He slept on a stove built of stone to warm his shivering body. These were before the days of immunization and medications that would relieve the illness. Another experience was that of a theft which took place when he was about twelve years old. He was very hungry and told of being in the market place where he could not resist the sight of homemade loaves of rye bread. Biding his time, when he was certain no one was aware, he quickly placed a round loaf of the freshly baked bread under each of the sides of his coat and ran home as fast as he could.

The relatives with whom he and his younger brother were left expected the boys to do chores for them, to earn their keep. No transportation was available for the boys to be sent to schools located in larger villages or towns which would have let them continue and receive a higher education.

Yet, now in America, Anton was still limited. It seemed that Anton had not left his village behind, but rather that he had taken the village with him. Without an American education, or even a rudimentary mastery of English, he could not aspire to the type of vocation which he dreamed to attain. Carrie remembered his drawing configurations on papers and telling her he would like to become an electrician. But his work on the railroad listed him merely as a "carmen's helper." In between passenger transports, he, like his father before him, was assigned the tasks of cleaning passenger cars. Sometimes they unloaded boxcars. American corporations were manufacturing items wanted by towns and cities throughout the nation. It was immigrants like Anton and his co-workers who helped to supply them.

****

The night nurse, the one who was on from eleven p.m. till seven a.m, interrupted Carrie's reminiscence. Had three more hours actually elapsed? Matt had gone. So had the nurse who earlier had promised to get in touch with him if more intense labor resumed. If Carrie wanted to protest the next shot, she was easily over-ruled. Doctor's orders. If she was hungry, there was the offer of sherbet, for she was in a state of labor. No more sherbet!

But now after the nurse completed her mission, Carrie lay awake. Again her mind was crowded with thoughts. She had always been curious, and since she returned to school when Matt was selling on the road and Timmy was three, she used written assignments in English classes as vehicles to research her areas of interest. In particular, she wanted to learn more about her parents' homeland. What had brought her parents here, to the United States? At one point she had written her father to inquire about her own mother's people, for except for the mite she had learned from the cousins in the suburb, she knew almost nothing.

When Anton replied, he explained that Maria was the oldest of four sisters. Maria's father was the village veterinarian, "a horse-doctor." He had returned from military service after World War I with a kidney ailment which eventually took his young life. He and his wife did have another child, a son, who died later, at the beginning of World War II.

Maria came to the United States in order to work and help her family in Europe. Her salary as a children's governess, though modest, was sent to her mother to help purchase land for a home and garden. An aunt, the sister of Maria who lived in the older cottage, now occupied this land. Beside it was the home of Štefan, the son of that aunt and cousin to Carrie, who had married and become a father himself. He had written Carrie and her sisters, prior to building his home, for a release from the heritage, which belonged to Carrie and her sisters, but it was not practical to claim their inheritance. The amount of money they would have to pay in plane fare to go and claim the land was far more costly than they would receive, so Steven was able to make alternate arrangements to proceed and obtain permission to claim the land and build his home on it.

Carrie sometimes wondered about the fate of these European cousins who were unwittingly caught behind what Churchill termed "the iron curtain."

What were their lives like now? What a strange feeling this was, to know you have cousins on the other side of the world, growing up under a different philosophy and way of life. Newspapers were not always kind in explaining their beliefs or actions. Sometimes there was the threat of war. If we have a war, Carrie wondered, does this mean my children will have to fight against their own cousins, their own family members? Probably this led Carrie to make the decision to study Russian so she could teach it.

She recalled one incident described to her while she attended Slovak School. This was experienced by the brother of the minister's wife, an American soldier who served as a sniper during World War I. He was located on the territory of *Slovensko* in the former Austria-Hungary domain. He came upon a soldier who was desperate, kneeling and praying "Otče naš"—one whom he should have killed. But hearing this man pray the Lord's Prayer in the language of his own parents, he could not bear to do so. Instead, he greeted him and told him to flee, to hide, and not tell anyone of their meeting. Continents and governments divided these two men, but not their language or their faith.

There was another reason why Carrie was motivated to study Russian. It was during her first college English course that she elected to read and report on Pasternak's *Doctor Zhivago*. One key word attracted her with its familiarity: s*trelnikov*, the hunter—one of the many words her father taught her informally in his story telling when she was being comforted after her mother's death. It occurred to her that proper conditions would elicit still more of the language she had learned as a child. The college did not offer Russian courses, but a new fledgling college about fifteen miles away was offering studies there. So it was there that she pursued her studies in Russian. It was there that she became acquainted with Dr. Mudry, the kindly instructor who had come to America as a refugee from communism.

Studying Russian was both easy and hard. The Cyrillic alphabet was mastered quite easily with repetition. Many words were already familiar to Carrie, but accents differed. This made speaking difficult. Carrie could easily decipher what she was reading, but when she tried to speak, she spoke the language of her father's native accented sounds. Her professor was encouraging, often complimenting her on her written assignments as "being almost perfect." Indeed, she was probably the most serious student in his class of sixteen students. Dr. Mudry taught at the college without pay, for he felt that it was his civic duty to the country which had given him refuge.

Gradually Carrie and Dr. Mudry became friends. On the day of final exams, a horrid snowstorm took place. Matt forbade Carrie to drive, as she was now in her third month of pregnancy. His concern was not only for Carrie, but the child she was carrying made him term this forbidden undertaking a "double indemnity." So she apologetically phoned and explained. The professor agreed with Matt, assuring her that when the husband who is the head of the house gave this command, it was to be complied with.

"You may come to my home on Monday morning and take your test," he offered kindly.

And so she did, meeting his wife who was hospitable, and who also agreed that this was a better option. She did not even want her husband to drive the fifteen miles, and expressed gratitude when he returned home after the risky drive to the college. The other students lived there in the dorms, so all except Carrie were present. But Dr. Mudry talked of difficulty in seeing the road narrowed by high snow and ice, making visibility very difficult. He checked her test shortly after she finished, commenting that she undoubtedly would receive an A. He appreciated Carrie's enthusiasm for the subject. She told of introducing the alphabet to her fourth-grade students whom she taught during the fall semester. The elderly man had the protective and fatherly type of countenance about him.

Now, with the semester ended, and having arranged for a colleague to substitute in the fourth-grade classroom, Carrie embarked on her studies at the other college, majoring in English, History, and Secondary Ed. Consciously or unconsciously, she wanted to follow in the footsteps of Durinda Hansen, her beloved high school English teacher who had taught her to love Shakespeare and Dickens. These added to the base, which Anton had formed, when she was still a recently motherless child and he related stories to her at bedtime. *Janošik*, the Slovak hero, could be compared to the English Robin Hood, who sought a type of justice wherein he stole from the rich to supply the needs of the poor.

Carrie's pregnancy came as a complete surprise. Yet she was determined to continue her plans, to complete her college degree so she could teach. She and Matt had set about a much different course from the business world they had left behind. With his summer course completed, Matt would have earned his degree. Carrie had another year to complete. She hoped this would be possible. Earlier that day, when she went to pick up Durinda and Timmy from their reading classes at the college, she sat on the bench near where the car was parked. Close by was a Catholic nun, dressed in her traditional habit. Greeting Carrie warmly, she commented, "I'm walking because it's good for the figure."

Looking down at her nine-month full abdomen, Carrie replied with humor, "But I don't have any." Then, after pausing, she confided to this friendly nun, "You know sometimes I envy you sisters for the freedom and time you have to study. I just finished my third year of college and have another year to go, in between this forthcoming baby and the care of my family."

The nun's response surprised Carrie. "You know, the love of a good man and a family are certainly precious. No books can take their place."

Family? What should a family be? Carrie observed other families. Some, like that of the Grandma in the suburbs, who was a loving mother, were lucky. Her cousins Lynn, Ed, and Lena had both their father and their mother. They did fun things together, visiting the flower show at one of Chicago's parks, the museums, and the zoo. When they told about these excursions, Carrie felt envy and loss. Why couldn't they do these things?

When Anton remarried, his attitude and approach to his oldest daughter seemed to change. Maria II had told Carrie, "He's going to be my Daddy now, too."

It was not until many years later, and some study in child psychology during adulthood, that Carrie began to realize and understand the background that had shaped the life of Maria II. Nor could she relate to her other than as someone to be feared. Unemployment, insecurity in those post-Depression and pre-World War II years took hold of Anton and Maria II in a way that seemed to limit their ability to even consider the feelings of his children.

Anton either went along with all of Maria II's ideas, or was not directly involved in making them. He was too busy trying to earn a living, to establish himself in his new employment, and to aspire to become both foreman and union chairman of his department. His fellow workers looked up to him and respected him. He was somewhat active in church work. Political conferences were also important to him. When the Czechoslovak government arranged for Hodža to come to speak to the Czech and Slovak community in Chicago, Anton was present at the meetings.

Carrie continued to do well at school with her studies. Teachers tried twice to double-promote her for a half year each time because she learned so rapidly and loved to read. School was happier than her home life, where she was surrounded by chores, which she did not mind, but the mental and social limitations caused her to lead a rather secretive life. All of these matters fully escaped Anton's attention until an incident occurred which he could not avoid.

Chapter IV
Maria I

I know you kissed me, held me tight
and tucked me into bed at night,
But though you're now a memory
Yet in my dreams you're real to me.
Though you're in heaven, Mother dear,
At night you kiss away my fear
And in the day you walk beside me
I feel your spirit tries to guide me.

Besides the two recollections of accompanying her mother at the church and pleading for medicine for her, beside her casket, there was very little Carrie recalled of her mother. Yet these memories, few though they were, remained vivid in her mind throughout her young life.

Carrie was fourteen and inspired by her high school English class when she wrote the poem. Somehow, while reading and learning the works of the other poets, she seemed to be inspired by them to write her own poems.

This poem was printed in the local periodical, the edition that came out on the weekend of Mother's Day. Carrie sent a copy to her former eighth grade teacher together with a note, telling her she was sorry for being her worst pupil, ever.

She received a reply, telling her to put the past behind her and commending her on her publishing effort. Carrie wrote other poems. One was a parody, inspired by her Journalism instructor, paralleling *The Night Before Christmas*. She had not kept all her poems, but she recalled this one, which was published in the high school newspaper. It read something like this:

> 'Twas the night before Christmas,
> and all through the school
> Not a student was stirring
> or breaking a rule.
>
> . . . .
>
> And after four years,
> Your head's filled with knowledge,
> But if that ain't enough,
> You can go to college!

Carrie tried hard to understand her friends. The girls she knew all had their own mothers. One friend in her Spanish class had a mother who was a widow. Sometimes she would visit her after school. Her mother was an elementary teacher, and, the way it appeared, her daughter was also destined to teach the little ones. So during their last two years of high school Carrie and her friend Joanna discussed their dreams of enrolling at the State Normal School in southern Illinois. Even though this dream did not materialize, both girls eventually became teachers. Joanna completed her teacher training at the city normal school. Carrie did so years later, after she and Matt had been married and had their third child.

It was then that Joanna wrote Carrie of the changes taking place in her own life and asking Carrie how in the world she had managed to accomplish all she had with all her family responsibilities. Carrie's reply appeared to reassure her friend, so now after a lapse in time, the women renewed their friendship and remained in contact with each other for the rest of their lives.

It was Joanna's mother that Carrie remembered. She often told Joanna how lucky she was to have her mom, even though her father had died. She also confided some of her family problems to Joanna, who related them to her mother. Both gave Carrie much word of encouragement.

Observing their relationship stimulated Carrie's thoughts about her own mother. Carrie only knew bits and snatches of her mother's life. One relative spoke of her faults. She wore clothes with a safety pin in a spot where a button had been lost. Another spoke of her difficulty in breathing during her final illness. One time Maria III reminded Carrie how naughty she was when she took all her mother's clothespins and threw them down from the second story porch outside the apartment where they lived.

Probably the most positive information came from the cousins who lived in the suburb southwest of Chicago. There Carrie spent summers and many months before Anton remarried. Cousin Anna and Cousin Sue both told her what a beautiful woman Maria I was—how she loved to dance and was always happy. She was the opposite of Anton, who was quiet and more reserved. Their description of Carrie's mother was far different from that which Carrie heard from Maria II and others in her father's family.

At age five, just a month before Anton remarried, Carrie was asked to be the flower girl for Cousin Elsie, another daughter of the great-aunt and great-uncle whom she called Grandma and Grandpa Fisher. It was a thrilling time for the little five-year-old. She remembered wearing a beautiful dress their family bought for her to wear. She threw flower petals from a basket as she walked down the aisle before the entrance of the bride. Her cousins had shown concern about her legs, which bore black and blue marks from the numerous falls Carrie had while running and playing on the jungle jim and other playground equipment. So the girls covered up both legs with calamine lotion. Sometimes she looked at the picture of herself with the bridal party with fond memories of all the attention she had received from these dear cousins. Grandma and Grandpa were long deceased, but they remained in Carrie's memory with much love. They were the closest family members of Carrie's own mother.

Carrie recalled how Grandpa Fisher made a swing for Carrie to play in his backyard, close to Grandma's garden. Here she could swing away, while Grandma puttered over her flowers and vegetables, as was her custom in the old country. She came from the town of *Myjava*. Her maiden name held only three consonants: *Klč* meaning key. She had suffered hardships herself, losing one or two children at childbirth, overcoming illness, and giving birth to six children who lived—three sons and three daughters. But she was always cheerful. For the first few months after the death of Carrie's mother, she cared for the little girl together with her oldest daughter, Anna. Later, Anna informed Carrie, at this time she would not allow herself to be in a separate room from either Anna or her mother. She could not explain the loss she felt but manifested the need to be with one or the other woman at all times, except while sleeping.

Carrie remembered the warmth of Grandma's kitchen. Impressed on her memory was the beautiful porcelain canister set placed on two shelves above Grandma's stove. This had been an anniversary gift the Fishers had received on their twentieth anniversary in 1928. After Grandma passed away, Cousin Anna gave the entire set to Carrie as a memory gift from Grandma. Matt arranged for a special shelf in the kitchen for the set to be displayed. It was a permanent reminder to Carrie of the love she did receive from the Fisher family in her early childhood when, motherless, they cared for her in a very special way.

She was a mischief, but forgiven. One time she placed the card for the ice-man in the front window after Grandma had told her ice was not needed, for she had adequate ice for several days. When the iceman carried another unwanted block, the child's folly was discovered. With a twinkle in his eye, the ice-man addressed the naughty child, "Now, who will pay me for this ice?" Yet he willingly returned it to his truck for the next customer.

Grandma scolded, but hugged the little girl as well.

Matt had returned to school, and their funds were modest when Grandma died, so they borrowed from his school funds to attend the funeral, which was in the suburban church almost 200 miles away. Their car broke down en route, and they were forced to use the borrowed funds to rent a car in order to continue their journey. They arrived at the end of the funeral service, just as the guild sisters accompanied the coffin exiting from the church. There was to be a gravesite service following. Carrie and Matt drove in the funeral procession accompanied by an elderly woman who talked the whole time. Chatting away in Slovak, she enumerated the virtues of the deceased and the trials she had endured with her husband who she believed was a tyrant. What a *klebetnica*! Gossip!

At the gravesite, as family and friends gathered, Carrie walked close to the coffin where the minister was standing, awaiting the beginning of the burial service. Carrie explained to him, "I'm so sorry we arrived late for the service, and I didn't get a chance to be there while she was lying in state."

Listening empathetically, the minister responded by signaling the undertaker. Moments later, the undertaker called Carrie to the casket which he opened so Carrie could view the body of this lady who had been so dear to her. "May I kiss her goodbye?" she asked, and the pastor nodded. He seemed to know that Carrie needed this closure.

Mike Fisher was now alone. When Carrie came to visit him the summer before, she sang songs with him and they talked in the native tongue, which made him so proud. Fisher was not his native name. It was translated from his native name, which meant Fisher. When he arrived in America, the people at the border changed it. This had happened to others who came to America so their names would be Anglo-Saxon and easier to understand.

One man who came from the town of *Trenčin* was given the name of Trenshaw to identify him. One bit of advice old Mike gave to Carrie was the importance of relating to people in their native language. He could greet people with a *hello* and *how are you today* in Hungarian, German, Italian, Polish, as well as Slovak and Czech. His work as a laborer brought him into contact with many immigrants, from whom he learned their words of greeting.

Old Mike died in January. His daughter phoned, but Carrie was already pregnant with this, her soon to be born fourth child, and Cousin Sue did not urge her to attend, as she was already concerned about her health. Yet Carrie did have other news to share. For Christmas she had received a bag of dried mushrooms from her mother's sister in *Klatova Nova Vec*, the family village in Europe.

An acquaintance cautioned Carrie. This might be a "commie

trick." So Carrie, friendly with a Latvian emigre, brought the bag of mushrooms to her office. Sylvia knew these mushrooms. She picked one up and ate it, just as it was, claiming, "These are the noblest of all European mushrooms."

How did her aunt, another Anna, and the second sister of Carrie's mother, know where to send them? She had been in contact with cousin Mike Fisher. Cousin Mike had continued correspondence with his family there, and had forwarded Carrie's address to her. An older sister of Cousin Mike's lived in *Nitranska Streda*, not far from their family church. Although she had been born in the United States, she chose to return to her homeland where she raised her children, and was to reside with them there for the remainder of her life.

****

What time was it? Carrie was roused from her reverie by the night nurse. She took Carrie's pulse and blood pressure, and read the results with the light from a pocket flashlight. "How are the pains?" When Carrie replied that she did not feel anything, the nurse informed her she would be given another shot. This time Carrie did not protest. She just wanted it to get all over with. Was this to be the third shot or the fourth? She couldn't remember and fell into what some call a "twilight sleep."

If it was true, and to some extent it was, as Carrie was to witness and learn from two of old Mike's children, that he could be very tyrannical, none of this mood was ever shown towards Carrie. She was the grandchild of his oldest sister who was still in Europe, so he felt a fondness for her as if she were his grandchild as well. If he was strict with his own children, it was a carry-over from his past experience in Europe. The Slovak was part of a feudal system carried well into the early years of the twentieth century. Each village had its overlord, who was Hungarian. The Slovak peasants tilled the land and paid a portion of its proceeds to the overlord who, in turn, ruled over them and was to protect them. But the lord also limited them. Schooling was meager, sometimes provided by the village church and only at the elementary level. The attitudes consisted of sequential deferences. It reminded Carrie of a story she once had read about the Duke and the Duchess. The tale related how one day the Duke, upset about some matter, raved at his Duchess. She in turn, chided her maid; the maid snapped at the cook who nagged at her kitchen worker. Even the children in the household were severely chided for some minor activity. In Europe, meagerly educated parents emulated the treatment they received from the landlord, often passing it on to their children, in a forced and unwholesome humility.

One of Mike's daughters was slightly cross-eyed. His response when he realized this difference was to firmly tell her to stop being lazy and to uncross her eyes. It was not until later in her life that she was fitted with corrective eyeglasses. Another time he scolded her for not speaking to him in his native language. He pointed to Carrie, who had been visiting and speaking with him, as a model for his daughter to follow. This embarrassed Carrie, for she was fond of her second cousin and disappointed at the attitude of old Mike.

Carrie found herself confiding her feelings to Cousin Sue, who listened and nodded. She knew her father well, but usually kept silent around him, not wanting to arouse feelings that would create verbal conflict. But, at times, she explained to Carrie, one must speak up to preserve one's own dignity and self-esteem. It was apparent that Cousin Sue was more successful in doing so than her sisters were.

Another child of old Mike was his son John, who had married a woman from Minnesota where he had made his home. Carrie became reacquainted with cousin John and his dear wife Marta, whose family were of Norwegian descent, when Matt was assigned the Minnesota territory while working as a traveling rep for an institutional food concern. John had served in the Navy during World War II and was fortunate to have his company save his place of employment while serving his country.

John also remembered Carrie's mother Maria with fondness. He was able to describe her as a person who could win the favorable attention of his father who was her Uncle *Miško*. When Maria married Anton, John would observe their affection for each other and feel left out, as he explained to Carrie when she had reached adulthood. John, too, felt that his father had been unduly strict with him and his siblings. While visiting his family a while after he had already married and become a parent himself, he had an opportunity to voice his feelings to his father.

"You were far too hard on us," he told his dad, who responded with tears when John confronted him. The old man listened, then quietly replied.

"I had come to this new country to raise my family. I wanted so much for you to be good citizens here."

It was he who had sponsored Carrie's mother Maria in the mid-twenties so she could migrate to America. She did so without her mother's sanction. Maria even claimed assertively when her mother voiced her fears and protests, "Be it my life or even be it my death, I am going to America."

Years later Carrie learned that Maria had consulted a medium, and the seer predicted that she indeed would get to America but that her life would be shortened. Was this what Eva, the mother, had feared?

After all, peace had come after the hardships of World War I. Their people were now united with the Czechs in one country. No longer were they subjected to the oppression of the Hungarians, who had denied them the humane rights they desired. But social progress came slowly for the Slovaks. Their population was smaller than that of the Czechs. It would take at least the time span of a whole generation to prepare the Slovaks through education and training to assume positions of employment and government to compete with their Czech brethren.

Maria was twenty, the oldest of Eva's four daughters. Their father who had been a trainer of horses and served as the village veterinarian, had returned from World War I with injuries that never healed. The damage to his kidneys eventually proved to be fatal. Yet, before his young life was ended, he and Eva had a son. What Carrie was to learn about this uncle was that he had some type of medical affliction, and that during the Nazi invasion his life, too, was snuffed out. Eva once again endured this sorrow from the loss of a loved one.

Prior to the dominance of the Nazis, early in Hitler's leadership, she learned of the death of Maria. When Anton wrote her, he also made a request. He pleaded that he was now a widower with three small daughters who needed a mother. Would she please send another of her daughters to be his wife and to care for the three children. Eva replied, "I have already lost one daughter to America, and I don't intend to lose another."

Yet she had benefited from her oldest daughter's immigration, for Maria sent a large share of her earnings home to her mother. With these funds Eva was able to purchase a large parcel of land on which they built a small cottage. Their mammoth garden produced much of their food, and there was space for a flock of geese, a cow, and chickens, as well as pear trees and apple trees. And there were berries, plums for the *lekvar*, the filling for the baked *kolachky*. Poppies for their seeds and other flowers abounded. Eva longed for the daughter she had lost, knowing Maria would not be there to share the home which she had helped her family acquire.

Chapter V
Maria II

When Anton announced to Carrie that he was going to get her a new mother, she was happy. Now she would be like the friends she knew in the neighborhood, in preschool. She would not have to go to Grandma's house or to be scolded for things she didn't know how to do. How much can such folks expect from a young five-year-old? She remembered going to kindergarten and in need of a handkerchief, quietly told the teacher that her "nose was going." Smiling, the teacher reacted, using her as a model of correction, perhaps, by answering, "Going where?"

Bewildered, Carrie could only answer, "out" and pointed to her nostril.

At this point the teacher got a paper napkin and then used Carrie's experience to instruct the children that Carrie meant to say that her nose was *running, not going*. She did commend Carrie for informing her so she could help her, and advised the children to tell her if they needed help with running noses. Carrie wondered, would her new mother do the same thing?

It was the day before Anton's marriage to Maria II, on the Fourth of July weekend. The ceremony was to take place on Sunday. Saturday afternoon found all the family busily engaged in preparations for the reception, which was to take place in the same apartment that had been Carrie's and Anton's home when her mother was alive and afterwards. This would also be the home of Anton and his new bride.

Carrie was playing with the other children, her cousins, and the new cousin she would now have, the son of Maria II's sister, whose approach to Carrie was to tease her mercilessly. Carrie's voice rose in protest. Maria II decided that Carrie needed a nap. She led her into the bedroom and told her to lie down. Carrie complied, but she was too excited to fall asleep.

However, this is what she was supposed to do. So when about ten minutes later she heard the bedroom door being open ajar, she kept her eyes closed.

"See, what did I tell you?" Maria II triumphantly announced that she was certain that Carrie had needed this nap.

That was only the first deception. Yet, for a while after the marriage took place, Carrie tried to please Maria II. At this time Anton was working and this left the new wife and his daughter alone each day. The summer passed uneventfully, and soon it was time for school to start.

Maria II accompanied Carrie to school in order to register her and arrange for her enrollment. Carrie's birthday came late in the fall, just under the deadline of the time that would require her to wait another semester before entering first grade. The two, Carrie and Maria II, observed the kindergarten room. Maria II decided Carrie needed more than "play" as was demonstrated here. The teacher surveying Carrie's progress of the previous year must have agreed, for they enrolled Carrie into first grade. Later, she wondered if Maria had really wanted her to be occupied at school for the entire day instead of only half-day as a kindergartner.

When Carrie brought her first picture home, Maria proudly hung it up on the kitchen wall. Art was something Carrie enjoyed. She was always happy when time was allotted for drawing at school. Much of each morning was spent in coloring circles of milk bottle caps, an old-fashioned way of developing coordination for children in the early grades during the 1930s. Carrie found school interesting. Learning to read opened new vistas for her. Not only was she learning to read in English, but also on Saturday morning she attended the church school where the pastor taught the children catechism and church history—and—in the native language. Anton tutored his daughter in Slovak, augmenting the lessons assigned at the church school. He also taught her the basic segments of Luther's catechism: The Lord's Prayer, the Ten Commandments, and the Apostles' Creed. Each night, at bedtime, Carrie was required to recite all three before Anton bid her goodnight. Anton's interest in his daughter had now evolved in a new way.

His marriage changed his relationship with his daughter. The snuggling and closeness she experienced earlier, during her infant years and those years after the death of Maria I no longer took place. Maria II had now replaced the little girl. Other changes took place in the lives of his family within the next few years.

Almost a year after their marriage, Anton and Maria II had a daughter, Ria. It was with great excitement that Carrie related the arrival of this new baby sister to her teacher in the last half of first grade. Her teacher smiled and nodded knowingly, for the pregnant Maria II had attended a parent's conference shortly before little Ria was born. In the thirties women were required to be hospitalized for ten days after giving birth. Maria II's absence meant that Carrie spent the time after school with Grandma Anna until Anton arrived home from work.

Carrie was glad to have this new baby sister, and she was glad that Maria II was home now. Until now, there were only a few hints from other members of Grandma's household that were like seeds sown for discord in the forthcoming years. Uncle Jan complained once when Carrie was boisterous, that she was learning bad habits from her new mother. Unfortunately, these negative remarks multiplied.

Jan, the youngest of Grandma Anna's three living sons, did not seem to like Carrie very much. She recalled how when she was walking across the street on her way home from kindergarten during the previous year, a car turned the corner and, approaching her, stopped abruptly. Just then she looked up and saw Jan walking on the street opposite. He had viewed the incident. On the following day, he blurted out as Carrie was eating her lunch in Grandma's kitchen, "Too bad that car didn't do away with you yesterday."

Carrie felt guilty. She had looked both ways before crossing the street and had followed the leading of the patrol boy. Neither had anticipated a car turning unto her path. Carrie wondered, why doesn't Uncle like me? What she was to realize in future years was that Jan, a victim of social and cultural disorder, was an unhappy person and an alcoholic. Periodically he would intrude upon Carrie's life and create unhappy situations for her.

How did Carrie's relationship with Maria II deteriorate? The situation came about gradually. During the fall, after Ria's birth, it was decided that little Milka should join Anton's family. It was never clear to Carrie why Grandma Anna was willing to give her up after declaring she would care for her throughout her life. True, Maria III and Jan, together with their little daughter, still made their home there with Maria III's parents, along with the youngest son, Jan. Perhaps they now felt too crowded with this extra child, whom they deemed belonged with her father and his new wife. Milka was still three, and, together with Carrie and her new daughter, Maria II now had the care of three children.

During the following spring Betka's godfather died. This meant that his widow would now have to work outside the home in order to earn her living. So she approached Anton about returning his second daughter to him. By the time Ria was a year old, Maria had the care of all four daughters. The close proximity of their dwellings lent itself to minimal privacy. Anton and his family occupied the apartment above the garage located in the second building behind the two story where his parents lived. For a long time their daughter, whom Carrie labeled Maria III and considered one of the dominant figures in her young life, lived there with her husband Jan and young daughter Anna, and as already noted, the youngest son, another Jan, also lived with them.

The situation might have been tolerable if Anton's employment had been dependable. At this time he first received word that his forty-hour week would be reduced to three days, or twenty-four hours. This continued for a time and then changed to two days a week, and then to *on call*. The railroad chose to limit his employment, which was his livelihood, to the amount of time the management felt he was needed. Was there a shortage of travelers on their trains? People spoke of hard times, of the Depression.

Carrie recalled how her father walked the streets from one business to another, making applications for work. She also recalled the visit from their pastor at Christmas with gift boxes filled with sweaters, knit caps, and scarves. Clothes were often hand-me-downs from Maria's former employers, although she did try to purchase items such as coats for each as money became available. One time she received a check from the bank, which had gone into receivership with all of her life's savings, and Carrie remembered she bought her a new coat. When she outgrew it, Betka would wear it, then Milka. Each was cautioned to take care of the outerwear. Need and warmth for the winter ruled over style or personal selection by the children themselves. These were still post-Depression days. The children were constantly reminded that money was scarce.

Somehow Maria II attempted to live within their meager income. Anton arranged to omit rent payments temporarily with Grandmother Anna.

In his intimate talks with his second wife, he revealed that, for those years prior to his first marriage and during his time as a widower, he had given most of his paycheck to his mother for her to "save" for him. Learning of this, Maria II prompted him to demand repayment. Anna's retort was that he would receive *her money* after she died. This was her promise. She had other children to consider, she reminded him. Yet the others had not made the contributions that Anton had made during those years. The resentments grew, and the children, especially Carrie, absorbed the conflict.

A regressive trait? Or was this a learned behavior shaped by the depravity of her childhood? Maria II and her younger sister were orphaned as infants. They, like Anton, also lived through the ravages of World War I while being cared for by their grandmother. Peasantry was not respected or educated in the manner which later generations in America would be. Carrie often heard her stepmother claim, "My grandmother spanked me so I would behave."

And so the pattern was repeated. There were times when Carrie dreaded coming home from school. She was uncertain what mood would be in play. Her life was a dichotomy. She loved school and learning. Probably by the time she completed third grade she had already surpassed Maria II as well as Anton in academic learning. But her expressions were stifled. What she had learned in school was difficult to apply at home. The rare opportunities Anton had to hear Carrie recite an assignment made him proud. To Maria II it was at best, competition, at worst, a threat.

"We all have happy faces because we're eating ice cream," Carrie stated one Sunday afternoon after receiving a rare treat.

"You should be happy and satisfied without ice cream," her stepmother countered. This response was mild, compared to many others.

When Carrie was being complimented for relating a story in Sunday school by one of the teachers present, Maria II accused her of "showing off."

Carrie, who loved to draw, would sometimes indulge in the artwork she had been taught at school. Even though Carrie's assigned chores—dishes, cleaning or help for meals, potato and carrot scrubbing—were done, Maria called her art work a waste of time, a waste of paper, often tearing it up and forbidding her to continue.

But continue she did. Betka loved paper dolls, and Carrie not only drew the dolls for her, but a whole wardrobe of clothes she copied from magazines she saw at the library at school. With her paper dolls Betka would role-play, acting out little dramatic incidents or ordinary activities of everyday life. Often Milka would join her, and the two would interact, pretending. Although Carrie enjoyed making the dolls and clothes, she never showed an interest in "blaying," as Betka termed their fantasies.

The three girls slept in the same room. Carrie doubled with Betka in the large bed, and Milka in her own twin bed. On hot summer evenings in Chicago, they often watched out their bedroom window that took their interest across the alley into the backyard of their Italian neighbors, whose home faced the street on the block parallel and to the south of them. There the Italian men in the neighborhood would spend evenings playing *batcho*. One by one, the girls fell asleep after they could hold their eyes open no longer.

Sometimes they had funny stories to exchange. If they became too noisy for the ears of Maria II, they were threatened with spankings. So they whispered, laughing at silly things they experienced. Soap operas held their interest, for that was what Maria II listened to for entertainment. Once Milka asked Carrie the name of Kate Smith's announcer, "What's Kate Smith's husband's name?" When Carrie responded, "Mr. Smith," there were many minutes of laughter.

At other times there were sibling rivalries, not uncommon among children at their ages. Carrie would retaliate against Betka by tearing up the cut-out dolls she had made for her and some of the paper wardrobe items. A few hours or perhaps a day later, penitent, she would apologize and make new paper dolls and added clothes for the new character. How Betka treasured her dolls. Years later, when the girls had reached adulthood and were in homes of their own, Carrie would send Betka paper doll booklets on birthdays or special occasions. Looking back and lamenting her treatment towards her sister, Carrie wondered if she had acquired this mean streak of destruction by emulating the actions of the stepmother, who had torn up her artwork. All this was quite a contrast to the reception of her first picture brought home when she was in first grade, during the early months of Anton's remarriage. Maria II had complimented her and hung it on the kitchen wall.

Carrie seldom cried, but when she did it was like a flood-burst. Sometimes her tears were totally inexplicable. She was afraid to cry, for this could evoke punishment from Maria II. One time she cried when the doll that she had named *MaryAnna* and that was lying on the miniature couch in the dining room had a broken leg. Tired, Anton had sat down on top of the doll, not seeing it first, and smashed the leg. Carrie loved that doll. For a while Maria II promised that it would be taken to a doll hospital and fixed.

Sometime later she noticed that the doll was missing. Maria II explained that it had been discarded. Repairing the doll's leg would cost far too much money. Forgotten was the promise that the leg would be repaired. Carrie, who had already begun repressing her feelings, did not dare to state them. Were these tears actually for the doll, or was this latent grief for the mother she had lost?

Another time she was crying while reading the chapter in *Little Women* which described the death of Beth. This time Maria II caught her with the tears in her eyes. The book had been given her as a gift by her fifth grade teacher, Miss Elizabeth Slatzky, who seemed to be aware of the child's needs. Stating that this book was a bad influence on the child, Maria II took it away from her and burnt it with the trash. Could Beth's death have struck a cord of grief again for the mother she had lost?

If Maria II disapproved of that book, what would she have thought about the other reading materials that had come into the young girl's hands? Maria II had a neighbor who shared many of the magazines she purchased with her: *True Story, True Confessions, Life Story.* Hiding these inside her school notebook, Carrie read with interest accounts of experiences that were written for the adult mind. They aroused romantic interests for which maturation and time had not yet prepared her. Yet as Carrie looked back from adulthood, they fortunately were much more desirable than the tabloids one might encounter during the decades of Carrie's adulthood.

The reading of every type of material added to her vocabulary and increased her spelling ability. When questioned by one teacher while she was still in a lower grade to spell a word, the older woman was astounded by the child's ability to spell words at a grade level or two above that required. Reading also proved to be an escape mechanism throughout Carrie's life.

Like Betka and Milka, who would role-play with the paper dolls Carrie made them, Carrie lived partially in fantasy. She wanted very much to have a good adult-like relationship with Maria II. She privately fancied going shopping with her, having a baby for which Maria II would be the grandmother, to be given the attention which Maria II gave to little Ria. Added to these were the conflicting social and cultural experiences: the public school, the church school, the home. Unable to synthesize all of these influences, Carrie lived within sets of psychological walls, gearing her personality to face the issues each of these inset walls brought about in her life. A sort of secretive life was evolving inside of Carrie, a life that neither Maria nor Anton could know of, or even begin to understand.

Anton felt himself fortunate to become employed within walking distance of home, right across the street from the elementary school where his children attended. Yet he was placed on the second shift, which meant that when Carrie and her sisters returned from school in the afternoon he was gone. When he arrived home near midnight, they were asleep. Maybe a brief encounter on weekday mornings might take place before they left for school, but it was usually only on weekends that they saw their father.

****

Waking from her very light sleep, Carrie was unsure whether she had been dreaming or reminiscing her childhood experiences. Through the east window the late June sunbeams flooded the room. Actually, it seemed that the room never quite darkened. Was it because of the time of the year?

Scandinavians called it Midsummer's Eve on the previous week. The nurse who entered had just reported for the day shift. Greeting Carrie warmly, she spoke confidently that Carrie would have a lovely baby. The nurse's accent and her name tag told Carrie she was Latvian, just as was Dr. Mudry, her Russian professor. Something the nurse stated brought the response from Carrie, "… but I didn't plan for this baby."

Her nurse confided that her third son also had not been planned. "Yet my husband and I were overjoyed when he was born."

Her words were confident and assuring. What beautiful people these Latvian refugees are, Carrie thought. They understand human nature—its weaknesses in expressing with empathy—yet remaining positive and open about recognizing results. She rubbed Carrie's back, brought her a clean hospital gown, and changed her pillowcase. Then she asked what she would like to eat, sherbet or yogurt? Carrie was to remain on a light diet. Also, there would be another shot, which still created questions in Carrie's mind. She wanted to trust her doctor's decision, but her experience after Timmy's birth made her skeptical.

Dr. Prompt dropped in briefly, was much more relaxed, and certain that there would be results before the end of the day. They would not wait for it to be a firecracker, as he had previously predicted at the last office visit.

****

Maria II had four children. Ria was the first. Yet her second child, a son named after Anton, was not born until seven years later. By the time of his birth Carrie was living with Maria III whom she addressed as Aunt Mary.

It was she who announced to Carrie that her stepmother was pregnant.

This would have been the fifth child in Anton's home. Could they possibly afford this? Anton had been working steadily for some time. He had even begun to send checks to Maria III and Jan for Carrie's care.

The changes from the first year of Anton's remarriage until Carrie entered seventh grade in elementary school had seen a deterioration in Carrie's relationship with her stepmother. There was not only verbal abuse to Anton's daughters, but also physical abuse.

Years later, when Carrie explained some of this to her close friend CC, she was asked, "How can you possibly forgive this woman?"

"Oh, I have to forgive her now that I am an adult, but as a young child, I was not equipped to handle it. All I finally saw as an option for me, personally, was to get away from it, to start a new life."

Some of this idea came from the adult magazines Carrie read. But the principal at the elementary school, which Carrie attended, reinforced the idea. Already in the latter half of eighth grade, Carrie had the opportunity to serve lunch to the teachers in their own lounge. The principal, Mrs. Bird, patted her arm, told her what a good job she was doing, and then asked her quietly, "Are you going to live with your aunt?"

Carrie had not thought of that until that point. A number of incidents had produced a flight into fantasy for her which somehow compensated for what she had so badly wanted: love and affection.

Maria II cuddled and gave much attention to little Ria. Except for the physical contact when disciplining the older girls, there was little, if any.

Carrie recalled how one time Maria II took her hand to lead her home from the carnival at the school on their block. This was a closeness that she had rarely experienced. Once when Carrie, remembering her earlier years with her father, kissed him on the cheek, Maria II chided her for this physical contact with her father, telling Carrie that one does not need to kiss someone to show love.

It was more important for children to be obedient and do what was required of them.

The teachers in her fourth grade class agreed that Carrie should skip the last half of fourth grade and be placed into the fifth. Both Milka and Betka had also been set ahead, or what was termed "double-promoted." The difficulty each was encountering was the social pressure of being with students somewhat older than each. Children sometimes imitate to please their peers. Noticing their behavior, particularly that of Carrie, who had also skipped some instruction in arithmetic, Maria II persuaded Anton to have a conference with the school's principal and have each child returned to their former classrooms. New adjustments were now again required for each, after several weeks of attempting to adjust to their double promotions.

Yet on the following year, Carrie's fifth grade teacher noticed how quickly Carrie learned, and how easily she could become bored, and so she placed books in her hands. At the end of the semester she again called for a conference with Anton and advised him that she was going to place his oldest daughter Carrie in the higher grade, skipping the second half of fifth grade.

This brought Carrie into sixth grade, in the year when the country was to declare war on Japan, and Germany became its ally. Pearl Harbor may have come as a surprise to most Americans, but to Anton, who kept close tract of politics, it was a fulfilled prediction he made almost six months previously. He had watched the Nazi occupation of Europe, including that of Czechoslovakia, which not only saddened him, but was very possibly the cause of the nervous breakdown and death of the church's pastor.

Carrie recalled how one Sunday morning they waited at the church door for long past the time that they were to attend church services. Finally the sexton came to unlock the door. It was then that he announced that the *farar* had died. Carrie remembered this kindly man who had taught them their first English hymn and had firmly disciplined a conflict between her family and another at the church school. The newspapers reported that his death had taken place while he was at a downtown building. The cause? The Chicago newspaper reported: *He had leaped or fell from a two-story window.*

The body lay in state, with the coffin placed in front of the circular railing surrounding the altar. There were visitations by the families in the congregation for several days prior to the day of the funeral. Carrie recalled the weeping of the pastor's wife and those close to her, attempting to console her. The funeral service was conducted by several Slovak pastors who were from the congregation's sister churches.

Carrie heard the adults around her discuss the broken-hearted response this pastor felt when Hitler invaded Czechoslovakia. Temporarily the Slovaks, under the leadership of Tiso, were allowed to become an independent country with the understanding that collaboration was to take place with the Nazis. Just a few years before, the minister had spent three months traveling in this, his native land. Like many of his countrymen, he was happy at the progress that was anticipated under President Masaryk. Now his successor, Beneš, was living in exile, in England.

The death of this pastor who had baptized Carrie left a void in her life as well as those in the congregation. It meant a substitute pastor in the interim. The successor who was finally selected by the church council was destined to become Carrie's mentor and confidant during her teen years. She became acquainted with him when it was time for confirmation lessons, as was the custom for all Lutheran young people when they reached "the age of reasoning."

What Carrie remembered about the war was her own experience at the elementary school when sugar and coffee and other items became rationed.

Children were given free days from school in order for the teachers to meet with the neighborhood parents and arrange for them to receive their rationing books. Coupons were designated according to the number of persons in the family. Carrie was invited to be present at school to assist her seventh-grade teacher who complained that teachers are always called upon to fulfill these civic obligations. Another classmate was present, which made both her and Carrie feel special. The two girls were the top learners in the class.

Being a top learner had both benefits and drawbacks. Carrie was almost a year younger than most of the students. She was not yet in the stage of physical development that the other girls were now experiencing, and often was teased. "Skinny ennis" was the nickname given her by one boy who took every opportunity to tease when the teacher stepped out of the room.

The fact that Carrie was given the first seat because of her highest grades created envy among at least two of her classmates. When one finally acquired the first seat, with Carrie sitting directly behind her as the second in class for that marking period, she taunted Carrie, telling her, "I knew I could beat you." To Carrie this spirit of competitiveness meant almost nothing.

She would gladly give up the first seat in class if only she could have the kids like her, and be her friends.

School was not the happy place it had been during her earlier elementary years. She was embarrassed because she did not have a real mother, like the other girls. Her seventh-grade teacher, who had openly announced in front of the whole class, that Carrie had a stepmother, asked Carrie if her stepmother was good to her. Carrie answered *yes* because she did not dare say anything else. Was this pride or fear? Something of both.

Carrie watched the other girls, how they dressed and fixed their hair. A twelve-year-old placed in a class with thirteen-year-olds can be like a twenty-year-old placed with fifty-year-olds. Maria II would not allow her to curl her hair. Carrie and her sisters all wore their hair in straight bobs. Unlike her classmates, who were getting permanents resulting in long curly hair, Carrie appeared odd. Her dresses hung on her as one might hang material on a board. Carrie wanted to be stylish like the other girls. Something else puzzled her. Remarks were made by some of the boys who had been exposed to street talk. There were girls in the class who laughed at jokes that were told, acting as if they knew what the tales meant. Carrie did not.

"Don't you know the facts of life?" one sophisticate asked her.

Sex had never been discussed at home, except maybe indirectly. Carrie remembered how when Anton was teaching her the Apostles' Creed, he tried to explain the purity of the Virgin Mary. His words were limited. All he could say was that she was *pure*. Carrie listened, but did not understand. Did this mean that she was always clean, with clean clothes and bathed each day?

When she was in third grade, she watched as the boy behind

her, after finishing his required class work each day, would pull out paper and colored pencils and draw. One day he shared his picture with the boy who sat across the aisle. This time he added a special word: four letters beginning with *f.*

He bragged about this word and both boys laughed, but the girl who sat across from Carrie frowned at Carrie, indicating disapproval. Later, at recess she told Carrie that the boys were saying a *bad word.* Neither Carrie nor her informant actually understood the connotation of this word.

However, about a week or two later, Carrie was walking home from the bakery where she was sent to buy day-old bread at a nickel a loaf. About three blocks from home, she encountered a boy who was older, maybe twelve or thirteen, who approached her.

"Little girl, do you want to #*%*?" Innocently, imitating her informed classmate, she adamantly chided the young man.

"You ought to be ashamed of yourself, using such a bad word," she replied with indignation.

"Oh, never mind," and he walked the other way. Carrie never told either Maria or Anton about this. Nor did she realize the possible danger that might have resulted from this meeting.

At another time Carrie was visiting the younger sister of the neighbor who had loaned the magazines to her stepmother. She discovered they had run out of toilet tissue while using their bathroom. Desperate, she asked if she could use something from a box of sanitary napkins, thinking it was tissue. Not only was she answered with a rude reply, but also that evening the neighbor reported to Maria II that Carrie had embarrassed her younger sister, who was somewhat older than Carrie. That time Carrie was scolded but she did not understand why. Somehow she was supposed to know something about which she had never been told. Yet she was accused of having a *dirty mind.*

There was another matter that puzzled Carrie. It was a repeated reference to her biological mother, to Maria I. Anton had confided to his second wife that Maria planned to have five children by the time she was thirty. The complaint that Maria II had was that she had poor health and should not have had so many children. Carrie wondered, were we, my sisters Betka and Milka and I the cause of our mother dying? She felt guilty for even being alive, being in the way for Maria II. When Carrie reached adulthood and had children of her own, she recalled these words. Why did they consider it wrong for her mother to want children? And what of Anton, why did he blame his deceased wife? Wasn't he a partner in creating the lives of their three daughters?

Aside of the fears Carrie experienced, fear of accusations, right or wrong, fear of verbal abuse which she could not label until many years later, fear of physical abuse, there was also the blame. Anything that went wrong resulted in blame, usually on Carrie. Blame for a torn hem on her dress, when it was thread-worn thin. Blame for the loss of Maria II's purse, which the older woman forgot and lost after they had viewed a movie at the theater. Carrie was to blame because she had suggested they go see the movie about Hitler.

Another time Carrie was blamed by a man at the church who had observed all the children playing with costumes and masks stored behind the stage at the church school. The fact that most of the children were involved and Carrie had merely joined them didn't matter. The informer who had complained to Maria II would not have dared do the same with the others, for they had both parents who would have retorted that the kids were just having fun. But Maria II, who must have felt threatened, decided to punish Carrie for the entire matter. Never mind that some of the kids were older than Carrie at the time.

It was in eighth grade that she did something which she could not explain, but which caused a drastic change in her life. It was now almost two years after the Japanese attack on Pearl Harbor. President Roosevelt led the nation at war. One by one the young men left for the military: the young man across the street, the two sons of the *batcho* player across the alley, the young man named Louie who dated the oldest of the four Italian girls next door. When they appeared home on leave their uniforms revealed which branch of the service they had been assigned. Some had enlisted. Others waited until they were drafted.

Carrie's hidden borrowed magazines related many stories of wartime romances and marriages. Carrie's Uncle Jan, who was single, was drafted and was serving in the frontline when American soldiers landed in North Africa.

The neighbor who lived upstairs of Grandma Anna and who had

always been kind to Carrie, sometimes arranging for her to babysit with her young children, had a brother in the service. One day as Carrie was picking up the family mail, she found a letter from this man to his sister. Carrie should have placed the letter into the proper mailbox, which was locked after receipt of mail. Instead, she kept it. Opening it, she found it newsy, relating the soldier's experiences. Its contents were intimate to his sister, telling of his feelings about his training, his army buddies. An intimacy which Carrie wanted. She pretended it was *her* brother.

For several weeks Carrie kept the letter in her book, reading it over and over again. This was a *real* soldier writing to his sister, not like the stories she read in the magazines. Then somehow the letter was lost. All she had left was the envelope. She decided to just leave it in an empty desk in her music class. The younger sister of the soldier across the street from Carrie found it and showed it to the music teacher. An investigation followed.

When Carrie was questioned, it was by the police. They asked her where the letter was. She replied she did not know. The detective who questioned her told her she had one day to come up with the letter. Frantic, Carrie did not know what to do. She did recall the contents and attempted to write everything she could remember that the soldier had written his sister. The next day she brought the copy to the principal's office as she was advised, but as she handed it to her she burst into tears. Sobbing, she related the whole experience to Mrs. Bird, who took the girl in her arms and attempted to console her. Then she took her into the private powder room adjacent to her office, washed the girl's face gently, dried her tears, and told her she had already realized that Carrie was trying to replace the lost letter with her written message.

During the next few days the adults involved met with the principal. The neighbor scolded Carrie, expressing surprise that her trusted babysitter would do such a thing. She assured the principal that she did not want to go any farther with the matter or make trouble for the girl. Maria II also came to school. The principal sent for Anton.

"Your daughter has a very curious mind and she learns very quickly," she explained. "A few years ago we tried to help her by challenging her with her studies by placing her ahead. What she needed was to be exploring more sophisticated books to occupy her interests. Had she these to study, this might not have happened."

Anton nodded, knowingly. Yet the man had to earn a living for this family of his, and a wife to please. If he did understand, he was now trapped in a situation that was insurmountable.

As for Maria II, there was only one solution for Carrie. Carrie overheard the conversation with Anton after she was believed to be asleep. Maria II repeated it several times. "She needs to be put away in a reform school for girls. She is bad, and there's nothing we can do with her." If Anton did not agree, he said nothing. He only listened. Carrie wondered about this father who had been so attentive to her in the early years. Didn't he care about her anymore?

Many years later, Anton told Carrie that he reminded Maria II that he had three children prior to their marriage. Anton tried his best to forewarn her of his position and what it would involve. The reply Maria gave him was "That's okay." Her confidence was based on the premise that she was an experienced nanny and housekeeper in several different American homes, both in Chicago and in New Jersey. She cared for the children of professional people and took care of their households.

One Sunday morning shortly after the letter incident, the family was preparing for church. They were ready and dressed when a conflict arose between Carrie and the younger sister. Later, Carrie could not even remember how it began. One girl grabbed the purse of the other, dumped out the items it contained. The second retaliated. Hearing their raised voices, Maria II entered their bedroom. As happened so many times before, it was the oldest who was to blame. No effort was made to allow the two young girls, now aged twelve and ten, to discuss what had brought about their argument or to bring about a reconciliation. Instead, Maria II picked up a wooden clothes hanger as she had many times before. She punished Carrie with a beating on her back and arms. Carrie was the older one and should have known better. This time Anton was present. He looked on disapprovingly, but did not say a word of protest. Looking on, so did the other children.

"You are bad, she is bad," Maria II repeated in between administering the blows. "You are too bad to go to church with us. You have to stay here, all by yourself. "

And with this declaration, Maria led the other girls out, with Anton following quietly. They locked the doors and left the crying Carrie with blows that would become black and blue in the next few hours. After about half an hour of weeping, Carrie made a decision. She put the items back into her purse, and then went to the pantry where the large paper bags were kept. She carefully picked out the few clothes she wanted to keep and folding them, placed them into the bags. She had enough money for streetcar fare in her purse. Although the doors were locked, she was able to leave by opening the bedroom window in the adults' room and climb onto the porch built in front of it. There were steps down which led to the yard. Just outside the yard, at the back of the property was an alley. Crossing the alley, she entered the street, which turned off to another that took her to the streetcar. Boarding and paying her fare, she sat down until the conductor announced Aunt Mary's street on the west side of town. Descending, she carried her packages up to the home of Maria III and Jan.

No one was at home. They too had gone to church with their young daughter. Hovering by their door, Carrie waited. When they arrived home, Maria III greeted Carrie warmly, though she was surprised to see her. She and Jan welcomed her and Carrie tearfully told them what had happened.

Carrie couldn't remember how Anton and his wife learned where Carrie had gone or their reaction to her disappearance. Maria III and Jan's home was tiny, almost like a doll house. They had purchased it the year before after saving for a number of years by making their home with her parents, not an uncommon situation in Depression and post-Depression years. Having only one bedroom, which they occupied, meant the girls would have to share the dining room to sleep in at night. Their daughter had a sofa and Carrie a cot. No one seemed to mind this arrangement.

What Maria III was to tell Carrie a number of years later was that neither she nor Jan were adequately prepared to raise a teenager. But they were willing to try. And Maria III was not willing to have Maria II succeed in having Carrie placed in a juvenile home, the "reform school," which her stepmother had suggested.

Chapter VI
Maria III

Aunt Mary, or Maria III seemed to be waiting for Carrie to arrive at their home. She gave her a big hug and kiss, and taking out her kerchief, dried the girl's tear-filled eyes. Leading her into the house, which she and her husband had referred to as their little doll's house, she took her into the miniature dining area, and asked her to sit down, next to her. Carrie, in explaining what had occurred in her father's home, began to cry again. She pointed to her hurting back, and told her aunt how her father never said a word while Maria II beat her. Carrie also restated the school principal's query on the day that Carrie was serving the teachers their lunch.

Maria III nodded. "Yes, I had a conference with Mrs. B. I told her that all of us in the family knew that you had been abused, but each time we attempted to say something we were accused of interfering. So when this all happened, I talked it over with Uncle Jan, and we both agreed that you could make your home with us.

We certainly did not agree with your stepmother that they should get rid of you another way, by putting you in that girls' home."

The first afternoon everyone seemed to be happy that Carrie was there. Her cousin wanted a companion to be like a sister. Uncle Jan who was listening to the *Quiz Kids* program on the radio, commented that Carrie should be on the show when she answered some of the questions given to the contestants. Aunt Mary packed her lunch for the following school day. They discussed how Carrie was to travel across town, but it was not necessary, for the young girl was familiar with the route, knew where to transfer, and was not afraid to board streetcars.

The bruises from the beating turned blue, purplish, and yellow on the following days. Maria III advised Carrie to tell her teacher and the principal what had happened, and to show them both her bruises. Maria III and her husband now assumed guardianship for Carrie, without a legal procedure.

Carrie tried to recall, was it before or after her thirteenth birthday, late in the fall, that she ran away from home? She was unsure except that she did recall the first Christmas spent with Maria III and her family. All congregated at the home of the parents of Uncle Jan (pronounced *Yan*). There Carrie was warmly welcomed by his sisters, who kissed and hugged Carrie and had wrapped Christmas gifts for her. Popular among teenage girls during World War II were headscarves referred to as *babushkas*, and wrapped with tissue and ribbon, there was one that had a fringe on it. Carrie was to wear this scarf for many years, and although she no longer had it, she did still possess among her favorite things the other gifts the aunts, as she called Jan's sisters, had given her: a pair of lined raccoon fur mittens.

Sometime during the holidays, Maria III and her family were visited by the new reverend who succeeded the one who had died earlier that year. The family had missed church that Sunday morning and Pastor *Bohabojny,* whom the youngsters addressed as Pastor B., brought Maria III her new Sunday school teacher's manual for the first quarter of the new year. He did not appear to be surprised that Carrie was in their home.

"How nice you can visit during Christmas vacation," he assumed. Unlike the previous pastor who was childless, his family of five children often went on overnights to visit with cousins. He had not yet been informed of the situation in Carrie's family. He was teaching Carrie's confirmation class, which consisted of seven or eight pupils, mostly boys. Carrie appeared to learn quite readily and, until this situation arose, he found her to be cooperative.

Was it a few weeks or a month later that he learned that Carrie had left her father's home? Carrie couldn't remember. Confirmation class usually met on one weekday afternoon, after school, and some Saturday mornings. Unlike the former pastor, he taught the class in the English language. It was he who began to offer English services on Sunday mornings to accommodate the young people born in America where the English language was more commonly spoken. He did continue the Slovak services for the older generation for whom their faith was grounded in their native tongue. But the intense study and memorization for confirmants were still required.

One afternoon after the class had been dismissed, Pastor B. stopped Carrie as the others were leaving and asked her to wait. When all was quiet, he began to tell her why. "I thought I might be able to help you," he offered. His words indicated that he had become aware of Carrie's situation.

Carrie began to cry. Words couldn't come out. Her wounds from the beating, the black and blue marks had faded, and even if they had not, she doubted very much that she would have shown or told him about them.

In the ensuing weeks he was to arrange a meeting with Uncle Jan, Carrie's Uncle Adam, who was her godfather, and Carrie's father, Anton, at which Carrie was to be present. Prior to this meeting Uncle Jan met with him alone, and described what had happened to Carrie. Nodding his head when being apprised of the circumstances, Pastor B. confided that he too had lost his mother and had lived in the home of his father and his father's second wife. His biblical stance was that this woman was now the mother, the matriarchal head of the household, and he respected her. From what he told Jan, she apparently was a person who cared for him and his siblings as if they were her own. When their father died, all in his family made certain she was provided with the care she needed, just as they might for a natural mother.

A psychiatrist he was not, but he was a straightforward, caring clergyman, who understood young people's needs quite well. At the meeting with the other men in the family, he tried to explain to Anton that Carrie was the oldest child when his wife died, and unlike the younger sisters, she retained memory of her mother. Her needs and understanding them differed from that of the younger girls. Pastor B. emphasized the need for a reconciliation, and idealist that he was, advised that Carrie rejoin the family as soon as possible. At this time, Carrie strongly opposed returning. Why?

Anton and his younger brother Adam talked with Carrie alone after the meeting. Carrie found herself blurting out all the grievances she had stored up in her young heart for many years.

"I wanted curly hair. She curled Ria's hair, but wouldn't let me curl mine."

"The kids at school made fun of me because I always had funny clothes."

Did she tell them about the destruction of her favorite book, *Little Women,* or the pictures she had drawn? The beatings, which took place on evenings when Anton was working? The sarcasm and remarks about her deceased mother not having a right to have children because of her poor health? These had led to feelings of guilt and distress.

The early months with Maria III and her family were pleasant enough.

Anton and his wife agreed to send child support for Carrie. Carrie settled into a routine of school and home life with them, but there were rough edges that needed smoothing. When Carrie began attending the high school on the west side districted to include their residential area, she initially enrolled in a commercial course of study. However, after only a two-week trial of attending the classes assigned, Carrie realized that her selected course of studies would not prepare her for enrollment in college, which was her dream. Uncle Jan was hesitant to approve her change. After considering the options offered, both Carrie and he compromised, and she switched to a College Commercial Course. This would prepare her for both possible future plans. With the study of foreign language and history, as well as added classes in science, she could acquire the background needed for college entry. Yet Carrie also would study shorthand and typing, which would provide her with skills for employment. At that time the possibility of sending Carrie to college appeared remote.

It was Maria III who discovered when Carrie became a woman. She had explained what would happen, but Carrie was unaware of the incident until Maria III asked her, "Are you keeping something from me?"

A bathroom trip confirmed Maria III's suspicions. Stains on her lingerie were evident.

"I think you're right," Carrie agreed. Further womanly advice was given.

One day Maria III approached Carrie with news. "Your stepmother is expecting." Everyone was surprised. Maybe this had added to the woman's temper the day that Carrie left her father's home.

Maria II was still in the hospital with her newborn son on the Sunday in May when Carrie and her class of confirmants made affirmation of baptism, or as it was better known, confirmation. Maria III helped her pick out a white dress, and Jan had a small corsage of roses ready. Only one other girl with about six boys was in the group. Carrie watched her father's face, which shone with pride, as she recited her piece before the congregation. Her sisters sat with their father in the balcony of the church where they could view the altar. When it was Carrie's turn to receive the rites of confirmation, she noticed as she was kneeling and receiving the blessing there were tears in the eyes of Pastor B. For each confirmant there was a special verse given. The verse Pastor B. had selected for her was from Ephesians (4:32):

"And be ye kind one to another, tenderhearted, forgiving one another, even as God for Christ's sake hath forgiven you." It was not until much later in her life, when Carrie recalled St. Paul's admonition to the Ephesians, that it became deeply meaningful for her.

The following Sunday the confirmants, as was the custom among Lutherans, were to receive their first Holy Communion. Carrie, dressed in her special white dress, was getting ready for church. Uncle Jan took out her corsage left in the refrigerator wrapped in dampened cotton to pin to her shoulder. The roses did not survive the week too well, browning at the edges. Artfully, Jan cut them out of the frame of the corsage, and then gathered several to replace them from the rose of Sharon bush in his garden. "Now you have fresh flowers," he announced, as he pinned the renovated corsage to her shoulder. His gesture was something Carrie would recall many times throughout her life.

During the following summer Maria III urged Carrie to find a job. So it was that Carrie inquired in a number of business offices. It was World War II. Help wanted ads appeared in many places, but Carrie was often considered to be too young. Finally, she stopped at a restaurant. A dishwasher was needed, and the owner needed immediate help. She hired Carrie at once, and when the day ended, tired, but having a few dollars in pay, Carrie returned home. Giving Maria III her earnings, she described her job. She was to return there two days later. When she arrived, ready for work, the owner informed her she did not need her. An older woman was busily helping in the kitchen. Disappointed, Carrie returned home to relate her experience to her aunt.

Another opportunity came a few weeks later. A cookie factory needed packers. Boxes of varieties were being readied for soldiers overseas. The owners, who were short of help, welcomed Carrie. When asked her age, Carrie, who was taller than most of her peers, lied. "I'm fifteen," she claimed. If the owner had any doubts, he was not dissuaded from hiring this willing young girl. One more worker on the assembly line. Actually, had Carrie been fifteen, she could have been employed legally by applying for a working permit. However, she did not qualify for one at her age. She continued to work for this company until past Christmas.

The change came about because a government inspector checking on employers in that area required that all under-age employees have working permits. The owner recognized Carrie to be a willing steady worker and wanted her to get a working permit, but she was ashamed that she had lied about her age, so Carrie merely quit. Besides, she did not have enough time for her studies. Reporting for work after school meant arriving home at suppertime or later, and often she had little time and energy to complete homework assignments. Unlike her elementary school experience, when everything came so easily, Carrie found her studies needed much greater attention.

Something else drew her attention. It was the social factor. If

Carrie didn't pay too much attention to boys, some were paying attention to her. There was one in her Spanish class, a year older. He invited her to a football game, but being too shy to discuss the matter with either Maria III or Jan, she merely joined him after concluding work at the cookie factory one Saturday afternoon. Sensing possible disapproval, Carrie merely explained that she had gone to a football game after work. Was this the seed sown to conceal another phase of a secretive life Carrie was to lead while living with Maria III?

It would be many years later that Maria III confided to Carrie how very unprepared she and her husband were to understand the needs of the teenager they took into their home. By the time Carrie was living with them a year, the honeymoon had ended. Carrie's friends at school had dates, social events, dances. Neither Maria III nor Jan felt comfortable about allowing Carrie to participate in many school events. Maria III even worried when Carrie attended a youth meeting at the church and arrived home a little later than planned. Cousin Lynn was able to verify Carrie's presence at the youth meeting. So was Pastor B. Yet Carrie was met with suspicion when she arrived home. Chicago street cars were scheduled to arrive farther apart in time after six in the evening. Carrie tried to explain the time she had to wait for the one to take her home. Yet not being trusted left its effects on Carrie. Rather than trying to explain each situation, she became secretive again, as she had when living in her father's home.

Trust. Carrie was determined to treat her daughters differently. With Anna it was easy. Anna shared many of her feelings and thoughts with Carrie. With Durinda, things seemed to be going a different way. Yet Carrie wanted to relate to her with the same openness she experienced with Anna.

Sometimes Timmy required more attention than either of the girls had when they were his age. She knew Durinda resented this. They had changed schools to accommodate Timmy's needs. When the betrayal of the private school's administration was realized, Matt arranged for all three of their children to be transferred to the local district school. For Anna, the move was an improvement. For Durinda, it was difficult, for she had left a close friend behind. For Timmy, it proved not to be as helpful as they had hoped.

****

Carrie's introspection was interrupted. It was time for another shot, the sixth. Not much progress with the labor. When asked if she could walk around, the reply was positive. This might help the labor.

It was when Carrie was in her sophomore year that World War II finally ended. This meant the soldiers, including the other Uncle Jan, would be coming home. Family interdependence was carried out to help him adjust. Maria III and Jan offered to open their home to her younger brother. They had sold their doll's house and bought a Chicago bungalow a few blocks away. The unfinished attic could be converted into a third bedroom. Maria III's husband also arranged for employment for his younger brother-in-law at the apartment complex where he worked. Carrie remembered how the younger Jan, finishing his dinner each evening, walked to the pub a few blocks from their home and spent time reminiscing about his wartime experiences with other returned servicemen in the neighborhood. One of his favorite songs was *Lily Marlene,* and he loved to recount the excitement of his duty in North Africa. Often, he arrived home smelling of the excessive liquor, which resulted in strong words of disapproval from his older sister.

Sometimes he interfered with Carrie's plans. One time Jan answered a special phone call from a classmate of Carrie's. Choosing to exercise a didactic tone, he told the young man that Carrie was too young to have phone calls and advised him not to phone her anymore. Very upset, she retorted, "I'm going to tell him you had too much to drink!"

Robert had been a good friend to Carrie. Nothing in the way of dishonorable action had ever entered his mind or in their relationship with each other. It was boy meets girl in the music class, walking on campus together, and an occasional soda at the drugstore. When at last Maria III finally had a phone installed, there were phone calls. Now Jan II had spoiled things.

When Carrie talked with Robert again, she tried to explain. Telling him how sorry she was about the incident, he expressed surprise. He wondered if he should ever phone her again. For a long time, he did not. However, this added more to forming her secretive life. She did not set out to deceive Maria III, but felt there was no understanding of her needs. Adolescents are too self-centered to understand the needs of the adults. Besides, there was their daughter, her cousin, who sometimes joined in statements and actions that pushed Carrie further into her secretive life.

Karolina—that is how the family addressed her. She hated her name, though it was considered a noble one, for she had been named after that favorite king of Bohemia and Germany, Karl IV, or Charles IV, as the English called him.

Another boy named Tony, who was not a boyfriend, but as she described him to CC, a real friend who "happens to be a boy," came to the rescue with the nickname that was to remain with her throughout her life. She explained why she did not like Karolina. In elementary school the mouthy classmate who made fun of her would call out her name, and rhyme, "Karolina, balona, full of macarona!" This brought laughter from her other classmates.

"How mean," Tony agreed. "But I have an idea. Why don't we call you Carrie?" Carrie it remained, throughout her high school years with her friends, and on, throughout her life. Only legal documents carried her full name.

Post-war times saw many changes. Rationing ceased. Many members of the military returned home. The economy was booming, for the war had created a focus on arms production, which forced a shortage of many consumer items. One was automobiles. Uncle Jan wanted to replace his old Ford, but in order to qualify, one had to apply and have one's name on a list, and then wait patiently for one's car to arrive. This could mean waiting for months. Uncle Jan finally settled for another brand—was it a Plymouth? Carrie couldn't remember exactly, but all appreciated the comfort of this new car. Jan had to have transportation to his place of employment, which was far to the northeast part of Chicago, some eight miles away from his home. Now the younger Jan rode with him to the same complex, where both maintained the apartment dwellers' homes.

As for Carrie, she rode the bus to school. Cousin Anna, who was younger and still in elementary school, could walk. After the cookie factory, Carrie worked at successive jobs. For a while she helped file papers and learned to operate a switchboard at a real estate office. Another job took her to a tool manufacturing factory office. Then she worked with some friends at a Sears auxiliary office located near the school. Each change brought some new friends into her life. The interchange of conversations with peers and adults alike were meaningful learning experiences. When she learned to type at the high school, she sought a typing job. Two of her last positions during her senior year included working for the telephone company on a part-time after-school basis. When she needed money for graduation, she worked at a soda fountain on weekends.

But much was to happen before the end of her senior year. Carrie tried her best to integrate her separate lives: school, work, and home. It seemed that there never was enough time for all she had to do. The movies on Sunday afternoons were her greatest delight. Faye Emerson, Ingrid Bergman, those wonderful stars of drama intrigued her. She wanted to be like them. Boys had become interesting to her, but not approved by Uncle Jan, who always had the fear that Carrie might get into serious problems. Her grades were acceptable, but not the level of her greatest potential. Work after school took her time and energy. Sometimes there were chores at home: the floors to clean, clothes to iron. Maria III took time and effort to teach Carrie how to iron neatly so her clothes would present a positive appearance.

There were arguments. On her sixteenth birthday she wanted to have a party. One of her classmates was inviting sixteen people, eight boys and eight girls, for her special birthday. Maria III did not consider this possible. Yet she did allow Carrie to attend a senior prom with a boy named Steve, who Carrie had known since freshman Spanish. She went over Uncle Jan's protests. In fact, his two sisters, whom Carrie addressed as aunts, came to visit to "tie a muzzle on Uncle Jan" in defense of her attending the prom. When Maria III told Steve that Carrie had to be home by midnight, he asked, "But can't we have dinner later, right after the prom?"

Maria III shrugged. "Let's not make it too late," she advised. What was *too late?* Perhaps it was around 2 a.m. when Carrie let herself in the house and quietly crawled into her bed, trying not to be noisy. It had been a wonderful evening, even though Steve had to show her how to dance. Her dear friend at work, whose daughter had worn it years before, lent her gown to her. Only Carrie's gloves and shoes were new. She fixed her hair herself. Steve brought her the corsage his mother had chosen.

The dance ended, and the three couples drove to the north end of Chicago, to Skokie village where food was served at a popular restaurant. The January weather ushered in an icy road that night. Driving slowly and cautiously, all did arrive home safely. What Carrie did not know is that when she arrived home, Uncle Jan was not there. He had gone to Steve's home to wait for his arrival. Approaching the young man, he demanded to know where Carrie was. Steve was the last of the group of five to accompany the driver, and Carrie had been the first to arrive home.

"I believe she's home in bed, sir," Steve replied. "We dropped her off at her door about an hour ago."

"Well, that's not good enough. Maybe you'd better not see her anymore."

Previously both Maria III and Uncle Jan had become acquainted with Steve. He had called on Carrie to take her to sports events. Maria III particularly wanted to be cordial and hospitable to Carrie's friends.

After this, Steve graduated and enrolled in the junior college on the north end of Chicago. Carrie and he met secretly, but his interest waned. Other boys showed interest, but Carrie was in an undecided state. That summer she quit another job. She could not explain why to Maria III. Looking back on her experience at the bookstore, she realized that today her employer could be cited for child abuse. His attempts to massage her body in sensitive spots while giving her instructions in his office made her uncomfortable. She quit, but Maria never knew the real reason.

The summer before her seventeenth birthday and the last half of her senior year were a disaster. Carrie had a serious disagreement with Maria III, one of a series of disagreements. She tried to discuss the matter with Durinda Hansen, who explained to her that her aunt was going through a difficult time in her own life. This was not titled, but later Carrie realized she was trying to tell her about menopause. Maria III was besieged with headaches. Jan, worried about his wife after one Sunday morning's session, had Carrie pack some of her belongings and drove her to Anton's home.

"Here's your daughter, it's time you gave her attention and took care of her!" He addressed his brother-in-law in anger because he was genuinely concerned about his wife.

Anton was busily engaged in caring for his infant son, the second born after the death of the first. His surprised response to Carrie after Jan's departure was, "You should have stayed home to begin with, and then we would have bought a larger home. We don't have enough room here."

Carrie slept on the living room couch. She was left to her own activities, without any attention from Maria II. The younger sisters slept in one of the bedrooms, and Ria slept in the room with her parents and the baby. The crowded home offered no warm invitation for Carrie.

Her enrollment at one church's summer camp proved disastrous, almost tragic. They were at Lake Geneva. Carrie had passed the swimming class for beginners at the high school during Phys Ed for seniors. She entered the lake at the camp. The water was warm, and she ventured out. Following the procedure she had learned in class, she confidently entered deeper waters. It was only fourteen feet, and she held her own until a rejected date, vying for some negative attention, came along and upset her. Fear set in as she felt her body sink into the water. Somehow she managed to pop up to the surface and yelled, "Help!"

The camp counselor, a large middle-aged sportsman, came to her rescue and helped her reach the shore. She was not injured, but frightened forever. She never tried to swim again. Someone urged her to return to the water, but she could not.

The red-haired boy who had come from southern Illinois that wanted Carrie to meet him on the sly, defying camp rules, seemed to surmise her vulnerability. She overheard him tell another that Carrie should be *an easy catch.*

The following night, an aquaintance of Carrie's, another camper somewhat younger than she was, and who was polite, told her about his interest in stargazing. He was what Carrie later described as a good friend who happens to be a boy. He invited her to accompany him at the park bench after curfew to see the Big Dipper. Carrie had never had an opportunity to study stars, and so, after everyone was asleep, she put on her robe over pajamas to ward off the chill of the evening and sneaked out of the cabin to meet the stargazer. The boy was serious and able to name the galaxies. They also exchanged Bible verses. Carrie explained that she was raised Lutheran, and they studied the Bible, just as he had in the Sunday school at the Bible Church. They didn't baptize their babies, though. They dedicated them. When a person decided to be baptized, it was a "believer's baptism," and then one joined the church as an adult. He had a friend who was Lutheran, though, and he thought that his friend got good training with his catechism and Bible.

It was during this intellectual religious discussion that the two young people, who were sitting apart, and not even holding hands, were approached by the director of the camp and his wife. Flashlights in hand, they waved at each of them, then each was told to return to their cabin. The director escorted the boy, and his wife escorted Carrie. The next day both were told they were to be sent home. In questioning Carrie, the director's wife insinuated that Carrie's water situation at the lake had been faked.

"Faked! I was afraid I was going to drown!"

Carrie tried to explain that she and the boy were innocent in their meeting, and she defended him, saying he was polite and friendly to Carrie. She also wanted to tell them about Al and Jack, the two boys who wanted to meet with Carrie for their own unsavory purposes, but the director's wife was not interested. In her mind, rules had been broken, and results must follow.

When they asked Carrie where they should send the telegram to let her family know she was coming home, Carrie gave them Uncle Jan's name and address. He and Maria III were gone that week to visit his brother. They also refunded the money that Carrie had paid for her camp fee. On the train taking her back to Chicago, Carrie thought out her situation. This was so unfair, unfair to her and to the other boy. The two culprits who had created difficulties for Carrie were not punished and were able to finish their week at camp. She and the boy who was telling her about the stars and his faith in God were being sent home. They had not even held hands. What a farce!

From the train station, Carrie, suitcase in hand, took the streetcar to Uncle Jan's house. In his mailbox was the telegram that related Carrie's return from camp for "disciplinary reasons." After gathering the telegram and her suitcase, she again boarded a streetcar that took her home to Anton.

"I thought you would be gone all week," Maria II queried.

"I didn't like that camp, and I almost drowned in the lake,"

Carrie explained. She did not expect any empathy for her situation from her stepmother, but she did decide to go to Pastor B., and then another person.

It was not the first time she sought counsel from Pastor B. A number of times she had questions about theology. School friends differed in their views, as their denominations differed from hers. He always seemed to understand her questions and gave her answers according to Lutheran teachings. This satisfied her for a time, but then new questions arose as she exchanged theories and practices of other friends. Once she decided to visit the beautiful old Presbyterian Church on the near north side. She liked the atmosphere. A short distance from Chicago's Lake Michigan shore, she found the area inviting. One of her closest friends was a Presbyterian. Everything they discussed did seem to coordinate with Carrie's teachings, and besides, they did baptize their babies. Carrie decided they had the same God, after all.

Pastor B. listened to Carrie's story. He was sympathetic, but realistic.

"You may not have been doing anything wrong, but you did break a camp rule by being out there. And even though your robe properly covered you, it was still not conventional. Besides, those people did not understand you. Why didn't you sign up to go to a Lutheran camp? We have several fine camps which you could attend."

The other person Carrie decided to visit was Al's mother. She was a fine person, good-hearted, and one she had met before, when Al had invited Carrie to their home for dinner. She had tears in her eyes when Carrie told her about his attempts to have an inappropriate relationship.

"And did you give in to him? Or to Jack?"

To which Carrie could honestly say, "No," and his mother believed her. She also defended that although what Al did was wrong, their church held the camp to serve their own children first, and that was why they did not take any action against the two boys.

When school began, Carrie's senior year often took her away from home. Maria II and Anton were busy with the younger children. Sometimes Carrie was involved in the family life, but usually it was just home to sleep, some mealtimes, and occasionally, church. Betka and Milka also had part-time jobs. Poor Milka was in trouble one day.

Her employer, for whom she babysat and did light housework after school, phoned Maria II to tell her that a sanitary napkin had stuffed up her toilet. She blamed it on Milka and said she had to call a plumber. Milka was severely disciplined. Carrie felt sorry for her but said nothing.

Another time, the clerk at the high school where Milka attended phoned Anton. They asked him to attend a conference regarding his daughter's truancy. Milka told Carrie what happened much later.

"Daddy sat with me at the principal's office, waiting, and he began to cry."

He told Milka that he couldn't understand why she had skipped school. He had always wanted to go to school, and couldn't. Now she had this golden opportunity, and she was wasting it. After that, Milka said she never wanted to miss another day.

That fall a woman from the Bible Church approached Carrie, who was now almost seventeen. Recently moved from California, divorced, she hoped to find a live-in companion for her thirteen-year-old daughter. Carrie accepted her offer and moved in a room behind an empty store that was to become a restaurant as soon as the owner could arrange it.

Maria II was relieved to have Carrie move. There was no bonding there, and she was busy with her household. What Carrie did not realize was the sophistication to which the younger girl had been exposed. She had a crush on a rough-talking street boy whose designs on her were not virtuous. He succeeded in persuading her to have an affair. When Carrie realized the seriousness of the situation and feared being blamed for it, she approached Maria II about moving back home.

"No, you cannot come back," she told Carrie.

It was then that Carrie went to Durinda Hansen, who had become the Dean of Girls at the high school. She had to confide in someone. Temporarily she had rented a room at the downtown YMCA which had rooms for women on separate floors. It took all the money she could earn at the part-time job at Bell Telephone, leaving very little for food. She met with her sister and begged some money from Betka, who had very little money herself.

Durinda Hansen phoned Anton and arranged for a conference at the high school. She was accompanied by the school social worker. Both discussed Carrie's needs and his responsibility toward his under-aged child. When told this, he raised the options of where Carrie could live. Her aunt would take her back, or she could go to live with the restaurant-owner. Both Durinda and the social worker opposed the latter. Carrie did not want to return to Maria III's home. The strife in the family was more than she could handle. Yet Anton was persuaded that he must assume his legal responsibility as Carrie's parent. So Carrie once more returned to live under the same roof as Maria II.

Carrie did continue her last semester of high school. She had made friends at the Y and attended the Friday night dances there. The Bell Telephone office was downtown, not too far away, so her work life and social life were close to each other.

It was at the YMCA that fall that she met a special person who would become her partner for life.

Chapter VII
Meeting Matt

It was a Friday evening and dance night at the co-ed YMCA in downtown Chicago. The post-World War II crowd—soldiers, sailors, and marines on leave, together with students attending the various academic and training institutions offered in this large midwestern city—all resided at the Y. Some, like the young man Carrie was to meet, were here on business, escapees from small-town America to seek their fortunes and adventure. Carrie, still a senior in high school, sought this place as a temporary home after Maria II refused to have her return.

Ever adventurous herself, Carrie, leaving the dance floor, humming to the tune played by the orchestra, Glenn Miller's *Moonlight Serenade*, spied the tall handsome man near the elevator door. Approaching a bit closer, she noticed he was with a couple of other guys who were waiting for the lift to take them up to the men's floor. Smiling at him as she drew closer, his response was a friendly "Hi!"

"Nice dance, wasn't it?"

"I'm not a good dancer.

"Neither am I, but I try. The problem is I go to the strictest church in the world which prohibits dancing." Memories of the denial to allow the young people of her church to attend school dances sprang into her mind.

"No, I go to the strictest church in the world, and we're also forbidden to dance."

He explained further; he was from a town in western Michigan, called the *Jerusalem* base of his church. Having exchanged denominations, Carrie noted the smell of liquor on his breath. His manner revealed he had taken advantage of the more lenient drinking laws in Chicago than those allowed in Michigan.

Without inhibition, she confronted him, "I think you need a cup of coffee."

"I agree. But on one condition: you come along and have a cup with me."

Looking around, both noted that the Y cafeteria had already closed.

"I know of a spot just down the block, a few steps away from here, but I need to get my coat from upstairs."

"I'll wait for you, but hurry back."

Hastening back from her room on the women's floor, Carrie found him on the bench in the lobby. Ordinarily she would not have accompanied someone who was a stranger, but somehow she felt this was okay. They had already established some common ground: strict churches and poor dancers. As yet neither knew this immediate attraction was to evolve into a bond for their entire lives. Carrie realized she did not even know his name.

"I'm Carrie," she introduced herself as she approached him.

"I'm Matt. My mom named me after the first gospel writer of the New Testament. Middle name is William, after William of Orange." The last name began with *Van* and Matt explained that his father had come from Rotterdam in Holland.

"You're Dutch? My parents were Czechoslovakian. Both were born in Europe, too."

As they approached the coffee shop, Carrie admitted she was hungry.

"Let's have a sandwich, then," he suggested.

"They make good spaghetti. Very Italian."

"Spaghetti it is, then, something I don't have too often. We only have one spaghetti and pizza house in our whole town, on Division Avenue."

"Okay. But I'd rather have hot chocolate than coffee, if you don't mind," she countered.

The young couple found themselves telling each other about their lives, their families, and other interests. Matt had served a year in the Marine Corps at the close of World War II. Now he was in Chicago, trying to sell magazines to earn some money. The young men with whom he parted at the elevator had come with him. All thought Chicago would have more to offer than their small town. It was easy to talk with him, and Carrie found herself telling about her situation. She was a senior in high school and would graduate in January, just two and a half months from now, "If I pass everything, that is."

"You should have no problem, I would guess, but I never finished. I quit to join the Marines."

"There's no room for me at my house. So I'm staying here for now."

"Well, guess what? I came home from the Marines and found three little girls in my bed. My older sister now lives on the West Coast. She's a nurse, became a cadet nurse during the war. I guess my folks were lonely so they decided to add to the family. They're twelve, seven, and three. That three-year-old, she's something else. Now, there doesn't seem to be room there for me any more. But I'll probably go home for Thanksgiving and sleep on the couch."

When they finished their food, Matt, now fully recovered from his earlier bout, paid the check and suggested, "Couldn't we go somewhere and talk?"

"I know a place, just across the street and a short distance away."

It was past midnight. As they walked down Wabash Avenue and turned toward the Stevens Hotel, the wind blustered over Chicago's private lakeshore, bringing November's promise of winter in the air. Carrie pulled up the narrow collar of her newly-purchased coat of mock leopard cloth which shielded her neck somewhat, but left her cheeks to exposure as a hint of cold rain began to splash against her face. They entered the Stevens' lobby where workers were already cleaning and vacuuming carpeting, getting ready for hotel guests on Saturday.

They talked and talked. Unlike the boys at her high school, Matt was a few years older, and had the composure of a man. It was going on 4 a.m. But their talk went on and on. If Carrie had learned of poverty in the urban environment of Chicago, Matt had comparable tales of how a young boy was taught to cope with the rural environment in his little village in western Michigan. He had begun working at an age even earlier than Carrie had, for he was only twelve when his parents allowed him to work for a farmer. His chores included milking between eighteen and twenty cows each morning and evening. He learned to use the Surge milking system. He also planted corn and harvested the wheat that had been planted the autumn before. Matt drove the horse-drawn reaper. Bundles of wheat kicked out by the reaper had to be put into shocks so they could dry out and be ready for the thrashers. Then the bundles were picked up and placed in a horse-drawn wagon and brought alongside the thrashing machine conveyer belt. After being pitched off the wagon unto the conveyer belt, the bundles were aimed with grainheads toward the thrashing machine so the maximum amount of grain would be saved before being stored in the farmer's granary. The straw was blown into a pile situated close to the thrashing machine. Later, the straw was bundled by a bailer. The straw was used for bedding cattle in the winter. For all his work, Matt at twelve, earned twenty dollars a month and his room and board. On weekends, Matt's father would come to take him home so he could attend church with his family. By the time Matt was sixteen, when help was scarce during World War II, he was already an experienced farmhand. He now had an opportunity to work on a farm in Iowa. Here a great advantage for him was that this farmer had the latest machinery, unlike the Michigan farms that were smaller and less mechanized. He spoke of other drawbacks at home.

Boys in the village did not have an indoor swimming pool. If there was one at the YMCA in town, ten miles away, it was not accessible. They made do by using the muddy creek that enticed them when enough rain had fallen and was deep enough for splashing and staying afloat. Matt described their diving board: a large tree that had a branch overhanging the waters served them. Carrie listened with interest. Matt chuckled when she admitted she had never seen a live cow. Such was the deprivation of a city girl. Yet this city girl who listened to his many tales fascinated him. She was so different from the girls he had known. She wanted to hear more, and he wanted to tell her all about his adventures in the Marine Corps. It was now very late, and Carrie admitted a need to return to her room and sleep.

"You know what, tomorrow's my birthday. Today was the last day I was sixteen."

"Then let's celebrate! You have the most beautiful eyes. Yes, you have the most beautiful eyes I have ever seen."

They returned to the Y, and each ascended to their separate floor. They did not kiss, but Matt took Carrie's hand and kissed it in a courtly style.

"Till tomorrow night," he parted, exiting the elevator first, as the men were bunked on the lower floors.

Carrie slept late. She did not have to work at the telephone company today. After she had showered and dressed, she went down to the cafeteria for a quick breakfast of cereal and milk. When she checked her mailbox, she found his note: *Meet me at six o'clock at the same bench where I was sitting last night before we left to eat.*

Before they decided how to spend their evening together, Carrie declared, "I'm hungry." Matt was amused at the amount she placed on her tray at the cafeteria. It was more than she could consume, and Matt ate the dessert. They decided on the movie. It was *The Grapes of Wrath,* with Henry Fonda. Carrie remembered vividly the song he sang with his guitar and later she sang the refrain, "Just remember the Red River Valley and the sweetheart that loved you so true."

Later, she and Matt discussed the abject poverty experienced by the family traveling from the Dust Bowl to California. They were not expecting to become rich, wanting only a decent livelihood. The Depression years had wreaked its wrath on them. Worst of all was the necessity of the son, a fugitive from justice, forcing himself to part with his mother.

The movie ended; Matt asked Carrie if she would like a drink. He meant a drink at a bar. Near the theatre was a place that appeared respectable enough, although Carrie had not much experience with bars. Looming in her mind was the negative reaction when once accompanying her grandmother Anna on a stroll along Chicago Avenue. The girls were running in and out of the doorways of the various stores. One doorway led to a tavern.

"You must never go there," old Anna warned. She mumbled something about places such as this were a bad influence on her youngest son, Jan. However, with Matt, Carrie felt safe. They sat at the bar. When asked what she would like to drink, Carrie recalled what another older distant cousin in the family had told her: "Always order vermouth." This did impress Matt, who did not expect this young woman to know much about liquor.

Post-movie drinks ended, the two began walking back toward the Y. It was past curfew time, but Matt did not want the evening to end. He began his powers of persuasion on Carrie, appealing to her loneliness, which he himself shared. Women he had met while in the Marine Corps were so different. He encountered those whose backgrounds differed vastly from that of Carrie and of him. He had even proposed to one, buying her both an engagement ring and wedding ring, only to learn shortly after presenting her with the diamond that she had shared her favors with several other men in his unit. Disgusted, breaking all ties, he used the funds from the proceeds realized after pawning the wedding ring for partying with a buddy. He considered Carrie. Young, but a Chicago sophisticate! Wow, vermouth, and that movie by John Steinbeck, she sure took the cake, and this gal was a virgin, besides. Then he proposed they spend the night together. Shades of the previous night began to overcome Carrie. She was indeed tired, and asked that they return to the Y.

"But, I want to spend the night with you," he urged. "You know, I won't hurt you. I just want to hold you." What was there in his words that made Carrie trust this young man, who until two nights before, had been a complete stranger to her? Was there a longing to be loved and cuddled, just as her father had snuggled with her in the days following her mother's death? Tired, she succumbed. Matt led her to a small economic, but tidy hotel, where after occupying the room he had rented, Carrie almost immediately lay down in tired sleep. Matt snuggled beside her, held her in his arms. That he did not attempt seduction left a favorable impression upon her. When morning came, she had remained a virgin.

Carrie had indeed gotten to know the intimate Matt, the soul that was gentle and kind. She had not yet been exposed to his weaknesses. One was a type of naïve acceptance of others, some who took advantage of him. Another was rebellion. He did not understand the forces which had shaped his parents' manner of raising children—a strict regimented approach to Christianity, an almost forced legalism, which both Matt and his older sister, Beth, grew to oppose. They tried to escape. Beth took advantage of an opportunity to become a cadet nurse, a program begun in World War II. As soon as she could, she left home for the West, where she ultimately made her home. For Matt there was only temporary escape. First, it was enlisting in the Marines. Hiroshima and Nagasaki brought World War II to its closure just as Matt began his training at Paris Island. Discharged at the end of a year's service left him loose without gainful employment. Attempts to find his niche led him into a situation which forced him to assess his life's goals in a new way. Under the persuasive influence of rogue companions, he had participated in a plan which led him to near tragedy. Carrie, who remembered only their closeness, knew none of this. Before he left Chicago, she gave him her class ring, which fit his little finger. He gave her his gold key chain, styled in the 40s mode.

She did manage to bring Matt to her home at Anton's once while he returned to Chicago to continue selling magazines. He held the baby brother Stevie, born to Anton and Maria II, and made a favorable impression on Maria II. "He's tall, and your type, just the one for you," she declared.

The conference at the high school led Carrie back to Anton's home. School and work took up most of her time. She spent little time at home. There was the job after school, and the soda jerking on weekends. But Carrie needed money for graduation—a dress for class day, class dues, picture fees, the annual, and so many other expenses. Two months and then it would be finished. She did graduate, but nightmares for many years tried to prevent her from believing it. Waking up in tears, she would search and clutch her high school diploma to prove that she had, indeed, graduated.

Maria III and godmother Eve were present. They greeted her after the ceremony, and Aunt Mary presented her with the watch she had always wanted. It was a Swiss Buren, one that would be able to tell a tale of its own. Aunt Eve gave her money. Another aunt had presented her with a beautiful brown wool pinstripe suit, one that matched Matt's almost perfectly, in the 40s mode.

A few days after graduation she boarded the train to the western town in Michigan in hopes of seeing Matt. En route she became acquainted with a resident of the town who complained that the Dutch owned the town. "They are too strict with their kids who become wild," he declared. How this could apply to Matt, Carrie was later to realize. For now all she wanted was to see him and be near him. Teen crush? Maybe.

Descending from the train, Carrie crossed the street with her large and small suitcases occupying both hands, and entered the hotel located by the station. She registered at the desk, paid for one day, and bought a paper. Surprised, she saw Matt's picture with an article telling of his plight. She picked up the phone and called his parents' home. Matt answered.

"How are you, honey?" Then she heard a voice in the background, inquiring who had called. "Just a minute," Matt responded, and then, "Where are you?" When she replied, he announced, "My dad's coming to get you." And that was how she became acquainted with Matt's parents.

Matt's father gathered her luggage and placed it in his Chevy. "You must stay with us," he declared. "You cannot stay in this place, all by yourself."

Matt's mother took the young girl under her wing. She was so proud that this young seventeen-year-old girl had graduated from high school that she presented her with a gift: a scarf, and a lovely embroidered and tatted handkerchief tucked in a package with a congratulations card. Matt's mother had embroidered and tatted the kerchief herself. She told of long winter evenings on the farm when, as a young girl, she spent time on handiwork and crafts. Quilts were usually homemade, and the women collaborated to provide the winter-coping bedclothes for each other and their neighbors.

Carrie noted the orderliness in Matt's parents' home. It was early to bed and early to rise in the real sense. After breakfast, the two older girls were off to school. The youngest, only four, remained at home with "Mama," as she addressed her adopted mother. Coffee was served midmorning, with either a cookie or home-baked cinnamon roll. It was served with oleo; butter was considered too costly. Lunch was served promptly at noon. Dinner accommodated all in the family with the exception of "Papa," because of his unique working schedule. He slept until the early evening hours after which he prepared to leave for his job at the hospital for mental patients. So his evening meal was heated and served just before he was to embark on his twelve-hour shift, from midnight until noon. A kindly man, he spoke very hospitably to Carrie. Yet in his household there was an emphasis upon every person carrying one's own measure of responsibility. This emphasis led Carrie to take the bus into the city with Matt and answer an ad for work. She was hired almost immediately. Her experience as a switchboard operator had stood her in good stead during a part-time office position she held while still in high school.

Carrie accompanied Matt on a night out on the town, in a local pub, where she met some of his friends. The town, the friends, the atmosphere were all strange and new. Here at the bar, after listening to an off-color joke, she admitted frankly that she "did not get it."

One of Matt's friends responded, addressing him, "She's too good for you, Matt!"

"I know it, but I love it!"

Living in Matt's parents' home lasted little more than two weeks. When it was time for Matt to return to his naval reserve assignment, Matt's father helped her when she was ready to leave. Actually, it was directed by Matt himself. The elderly gentleman had approached Carrie, in keeping with his family's values.

"You have been with us now for more than two weeks and working for two weeks. You are welcome to remain with us after Matt leaves, but you need to contribute to the costs of our household for room and board."

Discussing the father's words angered Matt. "My Dad's out of line. Whoever heard of charging my girl room and board?" Then, after considering the matter further, he suggested to Carrie, "Maybe the best thing is for you to return to Chicago. You can get a job and wait for me there, for now."

And so it was that two days later, Matt saw her off at the train station where she had arrived.

She had promised to phone Matt's mother after her arrival, but waited until she had secured a position as assistant secretary at one of Hilton's hotels. A friend invited her to share a three-bed room at a women's hotel within walking distance of Chicago's lakefront and its downtown-shopping district. Her train ticket, together with her room rent, which required in advance, took all of her cash. A kind young man whom she had met previously at a 'Y' dance offered to lend her enough money until her first paycheck, but he asked for collateral, to which Carrie agreed, by letting him have the new watch which Maria III and Uncle Jan had given her for graduation. What Carrie did not realize until later was the high level of ethics this man held, for before she had repaid him the full amount borrowed, he brought the watch to her when he learned she planned to visit her family. He was later to propose marriage to her.

But it was Matt that she loved. She recalled his father's words before she boarded the train to return to Chicago. "You do not have to forget Matthew, nor he, you, but you are both so young. I was thirty and my wife was twenty-eight when we married."

Other young men asked Carrie for dates. One was almost eleven years older and a former seminarian, now an instructor at an electronic school. Carrie often surprised him with her knowledge of the Bible. One time she joked about being homeless and sleeping outdoors with her head on a large stone, just as Jacob had. He also was attracted to Carrie. He sometimes invited her out for dinner, and one time braved a nightclub, which Carrie wanted to attend out of her youthful curiosity. Until now her life had been quite sheltered. Her dates were gentlemanly, and Carrie openly announced to them that she seriously cared for Matt.

Yet it was a while before she finally heard from Matt. His first letter contained a poem written by one of his bunkmates. It related that he was lost, like a dog without a bone, "without you." The letter along with the poem told her how much he missed her, and how he longed to see her. The war was over, but there were many tasks which had to be done. Matt described the activities. Succeeding letters arrived from Matt's mother as well as Matt. No one had written her letters so sweetly and encouragingly before in her life.

Occasionally Carrie attended the large old Lutheran church downtown where the young man who had lent her money attended. He took his faith very seriously and expressed deep concern when Carrie described Matt's church to him. Easter passed, spring in Chicago was welcomed, and Carrie found an efficiency apartment that was located on the north side, just two blocks away from the lake. It had a kitchenette and a rollaway bed, but to Carrie it was *her first real home*. When she wrote and described it to Matt, he asked her to keep a steak on hand, for he hoped to visit her there sometime soon. But the visit was delayed.

Now and then Carrie accepted a few invitations from young men she met at the hotel. Her pool of candidates was widened when she switched jobs from the office to the elevator staff. Sometimes salesmen far from home desiring female companionship would invite her for supper. One gourmet cook at the hotel frequently brought her a Reuben, accompanied by a kiss on the cheek, explaining in his soft Hispanic accent, "I love blondes."

When she was short of money, Carrie found a second job, working as a waitress in one of Chicago's chain restaurants. Her day job paid only the rent, bought food, and bus tickets. She needed clothes. One day, seeing a lovely pink plaid coat in the window of a dress shop close to her apartment building, she decided to save all her tips for a wardrobe. A layaway plan and subsequent payments outfitted her with the coat and two new dresses for spring.

She didn't get to Anton's home very often. Two jobs simply did not allow enough time. However, she needed some dental care and found herself returning to Dr. Dobry, her former Sunday School teacher. When she asked how much she owed him, he refused any payment. "But I would like to ask you a favor, Carrie. I haven't seen you around church for a long time."

Carrie explained that she often attended the Lutheran church downtown when she was not working on Sundays. It was much closer to where she was living. He nodded, approvingly reminding her that her faith was the most important thing in her young life. After her insistence, for she had a strong need for independence, he did accept a dollar from her. The new filling was to last for many years.

Then the letter came from Matt containing his proposal for marriage. "I want to live with you, Carrie."

Carrie thought about this. She had dated others, but none seemed to appeal to her the way that Matt had. Yet, recalling the words of Matt's father before her departure from Michigan, she wondered, was Matt's father serious about awaiting marriage, or was he opposed to Carrie as a wife for Matt? True, they were both young, she not yet eighteen, and he only twenty, but during and since the war, many married at a young age. Whatever the reason, she decided to write Matt and test the waters.

"Before I give you my answer," she wrote, "you must first tell your parents of this desire. I do not want to take any step without their approval."

The answer came from Matt's mother. She knew Carrie had a stepmother, that she was living "on her own," and was eager to accept the young girl into her family. Yet she also wanted her to become assimilated into their lifestyle and culture.

"Matthew writes you folks plan to marry, so why don't you come here and live with us until he arrives home, so you can prepare?" Her invitation convinced Carrie it was correct now to return to Michigan. Saying goodbye to friends at the hotel and others at the Y, she found herself being given advice, pro and con. One thought it was gracious that her future in-laws welcomed her into their family. Another, however, advised that from personal experience, she should seriously reconsider, for she had done this very same thing: lived with her in-laws prior to her marriage. She blamed them for the ultimate destruction of her marriage. Now separated from her husband, she spoke of returning to him after his mother was no longer alive. "Your in-laws might ruin your life," she warned.

Carrie boarded an airplane for the first time in her life. Both of Matt's parents were there to greet her at the small airport in the southern section of the city. Arriving home, they directed her to the third bedroom upstairs that was to be hers. August melted into September. Carrie became employed at a department store, where she was shifted from one department to another, never knowing from one day to the next what her assignment would be. Personnel had informed her that she could not expect to receive the same wages as she had earned in Chicago. When payday came she was, not surprisingly, disappointed. She searched the want ads in the local paper, but nothing enticed her. Then, walking a few blocks away from downtown, she passed a wholesale hardware company with a sign in the window, OFFICE HELP WANTED. Entering the building, she inquired and found herself led to the office of the co-owner. Learning she had typing experience as well as shorthand, he hired her. The wage was higher than the department store offered, and the position was stable. She was assigned to type and write letters for four department heads. Her desk was in a permanent location, just steps away from each site. Like other employees there, Carrie was able to purchase many items for her hope chest at a discount. Since manufacturers had only begun to catch up with the war shortages, this proved to be a bonus. She could buy baking dishes, casseroles, utensils, china, and other kitchen items that had just become available in certain stores. An hour for lunch allowed for social contact with the other women in the office.

Years later, Carrie recalled an incident on a historic day that fall, experienced by one of the women. It was Election Day. *The New York Times* had already predicted a victory for Dewey. Knowing this woman was an ardent Democrat, the two equally ardent Republicans snickered as she entered the office, certain of her candidate's defeat. Her retort, offered calmly and confidently at 8:15 in the morning was, "He who laughs last laughs best." And Harry Truman won the presidential election!

Before Matt returned home from the Naval Reserve, Carrie moved to a home for single working girls about a half-mile away from her office. Formerly the lavish residence of a pharmaceutical tycoon, the estate was now under the sponsorship of a woman's guild in a Protestant church and housed twenty-seven working girls as well as a permanent staff. Carrie shared the third floor dorm room that had once served as a ballroom with three other young women. House rules to be kept included making beds daily; clean sheets were provided weekly and clean towels twice a week. Room and board included all three meals every day. Sunday breakfasts were served in the kitchen, for the girls rose at various hours. Most attended church, an unspoken requirement. Although most were Protestant, there was no rejection of Catholics. Matt, who now worked in town, often visited Carrie in the parlor after working hours. Guests were allowed once weekly, so he usually joined Carrie there for Sunday dinner.

The couple began attending the Lutheran Church located within a short walking distance of Carrie's home. The vestments worn by the pastor were a new phenomenon to Matt, who was used to formal street attire by the minister of his family's church. As Matt became familiar with the form of worship service, he grew to love the liturgy. Many of the hymns were the same that were sung in his childhood church. By the time their wedding date had been set, Matt felt at ease with the minister. During their pre-nuptial counseling, the reverend questioned them about their desired church affiliation. Matt assured him that he enjoyed the Lutheran services and that his belief was compatible. Carrie would never forget the graciousness of this pastor who emphasized to them that their choice of a church should bind them, and never be a source of division between them. "If you were strongly bent on remaining in your denomination, I would encourage Carrie to join it to be with you."

Since their families belonged to two different denominations, Carrie and Matt decided on a compromise for the physical setting of exchanging their vows. It would be right here, at Oakcrest, the place that had been home for Carrie these last eight months. They arranged for flowers and candelabra to be placed before the fireplace in the beautiful Victorian parlor, where the ceremony would take place. The large greeting hall adjacent to the parlor was suitable for the reception. To keep things simple, their guests would be served cake and punch, nuts and mints.

There was great excitement among the housemates. Many offered their help. One welcome gesture was that of a housemate who, when the veil Carrie was to wear pulled apart from the pearl-seeded head-dress and needed a seamstress's attention, lovingly provided it. Betka was maid of honor as well as the only attendant. Matt's friend. John, who had helped him select his wedding suit, served him as best man. He willingly offered his car, poor brakes and all, for Matt and Carrie to drive on their honeymoon.

When Carrie wrote Anton of her forthcoming marriage, he wrote a letter explaining why he would not be able to attend. Betka, who was to be her maid of honor and only attendant, visited a month prior in order to choose her gown and headpiece. Milka wrote, telling how sad she was that their father would not be there. The pastor who was to marry them offered to write Anton, if Carrie approved, to encourage him to be present at his daughter's wedding. Was it guilt or lack of confidence that led Carrie to answer him as she did? Recalling all the history of her young life and her past relationship with Maria II, Carrie replied, "No, I don't think it would help or do any good." Years later, she wondered why she had not agreed to let the clergyman try.

Yet, a close friend pointed out to Carrie that Anton did, indirectly, offer his blessing. In his letter, he referred to the marriage celebration, which Jesus attended at Cana, where He performed His early miracle, changing the water into wine.

Did Anton feel as if he were caught between the wishes of his wife and the needs of his daughter? Was it lack of money? Yet Milka reported that a new bicycle had been purchased for one of the other younger children that summer. Maria III also claimed he could have ridden with them. Was it pride that prevented Anton to approach his sister in order to share a ride to his oldest daughter's wedding? But Maria III, together with Uncle Jan, Aunt Eve, and Grandma Anna were all there. So was Cousin Ann.

On the morning of the wedding, Carrie discovered that she had not given Matt the bag containing the dress socks he would need to wear for the ceremony. So it was Uncle Jan who brought them to Matt, following Carrie's directions to drive to the street on which their future home would be. It was a small upstairs apartment above a retired landlord. They were given the three rooms, a bedroom, kitchen with dining space furnished with stove and refrigerator, table and chairs, and the bathroom. The landlady wished to keep what would have been the living room for her storage room. Earlier that week, Matt had secured the rent, and together they filled the apartment with all the items Carrie and he had purchased during their engagement: dishes, silverware, some linens, and the cooking utensils given them by Matt's parents. Matt as yet had no car, but one borrowed from a friend helped them transfer their belongings, and on the night before the wedding, he decided to sleep in the apartment, their future home. Uncle Jan drove him to Oakcrest.

Carrie had selected her satin gown in February, never considering the possible heat of early July. Her hair, though curled the night before, hung in stringy locks under the repaired veil, which had been worn some time before by Matt's sister Beth—an accessory that his mother had stored carefully after her daughter's wedding.

One housemate, a talented organist, played a series of wedding hymns, after which she sang *O Perfect Love*. Then the organ began with the *Wedding March*. Standing at the foot of the stairway and ready to lead Carrie to Matt's side was Uncle Jan. Matt's best man and Betka were waiting before the fireplace. Waiting also was the Lutheran pastor with his back to the fireplace. Candelabra graced either side of the wedding party. All was ready for the bride's appearance.

For about a minute Carrie felt fright. "I can't do this," she told her close friend who had introduced her to this home and had been her co-worker for the past year.

"Oh, but you must, you can't back out now, Matt's waiting," she declared firmly and gave Carrie enough of a nudge forward so that the guests could finally catch sight of the awaited bride as she glided down the stairs. At the foot of the stairs Uncle Jan waited for her and, taking his arm, Carrie was led into the parlor where Matt, smiling, waited for her.

At the close of the ceremony, Matt kissed her and whispered in her ear: "I borrowed John's car and we're going to Holland, and then to Saugatuck, where I made a reservation for our honeymoon night." He was so excited and happy that Carrie's earlier doubts disappeared.

This was the first opportunity for Matt's family to meet Carrie's. It was then that Carrie's grandmother Anna pointed to Matt's mother and declared to Carrie in the native Slovak, that God had given her a new mother now, and in a commanding tone, told Carrie she must appreciate her.

After the reception, the family all visited at Carrie and Matt's apartment. Carrie showed them the lovely silverware, which Matt had bought for her during their engagement. Uncle Jan had helped them gather their wedding gifts and transport them to their new home. It was only years later before Carrie would fully comprehend the great efforts her family members had made to be there for her, on her wedding day.

Before they left town, Matt and Carrie stopped to purchase

bathing suits. Matt drove to Holland where he had made the reservations at a classic hotel. When Uncle Jan learned that they also planned to go to Saugatuck, he gave them the address of someone he knew from his place of employment—a friend who owned a small resort there. So that is where they stopped to learn about Goshorn Lake. Carrie's swimsuit did not prove to be very sturdy, and a short time after entering the water, she noticed a tear in a very sensitive spot. Matt teased her about having to remain under water "to protect your dignity."

Late in the day they returned to the town and their new home. The following day was the Fourth of July, and most stores were closed. Yet they needed food and groceries before returning John's car to him on the following evening. Years later, they laughed at how naïve they were at shopping budget-wise. For the only store they found open probably charged ten to twenty percent more for many of their grocery items.

"We did survive, though, and we were happy enough except for outside social issues which we were too inexperienced to deal with," Carrie later told her friend, CC.

Things did not go well with their first landlord. Concerned that Carrie was not working, she accused her of using too much electricity while she was home all day. Within a month after many complaints, the young couple decided to move. Finding another place to live was not easy, but finally, on a Saturday evening, they located an apartment near the residence of their new landlord. It was less than ideal. There was only a bedroom and a kitchenette. The bathroom had to be shared with another couple. Just as they received their receipt for the first week's rent, another couple approached the landlord.

"See how lucky you are?" their new landlady retorted, as she turned the prospective couple away.

Were they lucky? Matt's parents did not think so. They had purchased the building for their store, and the apartment in the back was now vacant. They wrote a note inviting them to consider moving there. Not long after, Carrie found an office job and planned to use her salary to buy furniture. That fall, they moved in. What they did not anticipate were the expectations parents and son had of each other. Looking back, Carrie wondered, why did Matt feel this strong resentment at his parents' expectations?

Carrie was to realize, as those involved directly did not seem able to, that the problem stemmed from the top down. It was something like the situation with Maria II. The differences were the *top*. In the case of Maria II, it was the political set-up of Austria-Hungary. The overlord often abused the peasant in his domain, who in turn abused those under him or her, and often it was the children, for that was the method shown to the uneducated: force to the point of abuse. Maria II's grandmother, who raised the orphaned child, by her own admission, often used force.

"It was good for me, it made me behave," Maria defended. And so Maria II followed suit with her oldest stepdaughter.

Thus it was with Matt's family. The top there was the hospital, where his father was employed. The administration made rigid demands on the elderly gentleman throughout his working time there. He accepted this in a religious way, for one must not complain about one's suffering, but accept it, just as Christ had. Yet the end result was his relationship, or rather, the lack of it, between father and son. As a young boy, Matt was subjected to the rigid routine repeated by his mother, who, in turn, followed methods used by her own limited father. There was no such thing as child psychology applied. Only force. Matt's cumulative resentment now became manifest in his early years of marriage to Carrie.

By the time Anna was born, they were in their own bungalow, purchased with funds saved for Carrie by her aunt. Money was tight, but somehow, they did manage. What created insecurity for Carrie was the restlessness Matt was experiencing with a variety of job changes. When he left the lumberyard, he was welcomed back to the factory. That winter he experienced a terrible accident to his hand. The Riserwelt Machine had belts, which pulled his hand into the machine structure and tore open the muscles in the palm. Although the foreman took him to the hospital where they cleaned out the center of his palm, which had been pressed under the spoke of his machine, he did not arrange for Matt's transportation home. Matt arrived on the bus after waiting for its scheduled arrival and then another six-mile ride. Pain was excruciating. It would be many months, perhaps years before the tenderness from the injury was healed. This led Matt to locate other employment. This time it was at a large factory where auto parts were manufactured. Again, it was working the second shift. Years later, Matt was to ask himself why he did not use that time for continuing his education. He could have attended morning classes at the college while working the second shift. Then an opportunity came for him to work days.

This job involved installing asbestos on steam and water pipes in various factories and businesses. Holding this job meant joining the pipe-covers' union. By the time Durinda, their second daughter, was born, Matt changed jobs again. This time it was selling aluminum cooking utensils. What was in his favor is that these were years immediately after World War II, and items such as he offered for sale were very much in demand, not only by engaged young couples, but by many of their mothers and other women in their family who had not been able to buy these during the war years. Carrie helped Matt by setting up appointments, keeping track of books, and general office work. After he became a sales manager, they learned their third child was on the way. It was the arrival of their son Timothy that changed their lives in many ways.

Like many in the corporate world, the young couple was to learn that often their lives were subjected to a built-in bureaucracy that intruded upon their lives. Yet for several years, Matt enjoyed his work. Sales work brought him into contact with many types of people. The give and take of the business world offered him the challenges that suited his personality. Although many weekday evenings were taken up with appointments and closings, weekdays, particularly those in the summer months, allowed a certain amount of freedom to enjoy Lake Michigan. Outings gave opportunity for much attention to their two little daughters. Carrie recalled placing Durinda in an enclosed fence built of sand at the beach with shovel and pail while Anna built sand castles. Matt swam, but Carrie floated on the rubber raft. For the first time in her life, she acquired a lovely tan that remained with her late into the fall. Her tan brought comments from the obstetrician who informed her that she was to have another child in the spring.

With Timmy's birth came a change in living quarters. They sold their modest two-bedroom bungalow and bought a new larger ranch house with three bedrooms and an attached garage. The yard was very large. In back was a huge field, an area that had once been farmland and was still used by its owners to grow potatoes and wild asparagus that the children sometimes picked and brought home for dinner. Matt was elated with the birth of a son. What Carrie did not anticipate, and then feared, was a job change that proved to be disastrous to her family. In addition, she experienced illness that necessitated hospitalization and a long recovery time.

Matt's deals. That's what his friends called the job changes. Somehow all the desire for remaining in a "hard-sell" job was no longer appealing to Matt. He applied for several positions without success. Then a friend of his arranged for Matt to meet his employer. Carl was about to leave his sales position for one that he felt was more suitable, but in order to exit with favorable feelings, he offered a chance for Matt to become his replacement. This job would take Matt out of town and overnight many weekdays. He was to represent the company at institutional food sales. Matt called on schools, hospitals, campsites, and colleges throughout the western half of the state. Sometimes he drove home from the Upper Peninsula on Friday, arriving to spend the weekend with the family. This left Carrie with all the responsibility. With great effort she managed to assume this array of tasks, all the while still recovering from her illness. By the time Timmy was a year old, Matt had made his mark with higher than average sales and was commended by the owner for his aggressiveness, from which his company was prospering. Yet problems eventually arose. Some of the employees were aroused to jealousy because of Matt's success. Matt had not only raised the total sales on the western side of the state, replaced his sales position with a new person, but also hired and trained a new sales representative in the eastern part of the state. Then Matt was sent to Minnesota to open a new territory.

Going so far away from home meant separation from his family for weeks at a time. That year, Matt left after Thanksgiving and did not return until a few days before Christmas. Carrie surprised him with new carpeting on their living room floor. This allowed Timmy to walk barefoot if he wanted. He was happy to see his dad. In spite of his youth, he seemed to remember this important person. There was a musical teddy bear for him. There were beautiful gifts for the girls, too. A dollhouse-sized cupboard with dishes for Anna and a doll for Durinda were brought home from Minnesota. It was a wonderful Christmas. Matt had to have some minor surgery on his toe while he was home, but it was healing well when he had to leave the day after the New Year. It was then that Carrie decided she would join him in Minnesota as soon as the girls had completed the first semester of school, at the end of January.

That proved to be difficult. The World War II shortage of places to live and apartments to rent had still not caught up with supply and demand. Carrie and Matt wound up in a double motel accommodation just north of Minneapolis. The children were enrolled in the school there. Matt had to travel in order to establish accounts. Illness attacked both Carrie and her children. Though she phoned Matt, he was unable to join her as he had appointments for business that had to be met. First, there was the flu that resembled pneumonia for Carrie. Then Timmy caught chicken pox, and the girls followed; the pox covered their bodies and the bottoms of their feet. When May came, a new salesman had been hired to represent the company, and Matt could take Carrie and the family back home to Michigan. It was after their arrival home that difficulties began.

Now that Matt had successfully established three territories, his company offered a new challenge. What happened in the meantime was that Matt had been offered an opportunity to invest in the company. His parents felt this was a favorable investment and gave him the funds from their own savings. Matt was next designated to open up the New York area. Neither the company officials nor Matt could surmise the competition he would encounter there. Other long-established companies had been doing business there for years. Contracts were sewed up. Matt did not reap the same level of success that he had in the former three territories. Besides, one executive, an alcoholic, was having personal problems and decided to take action, which proved to be threatening to Matt.

They met in the boardroom. The cost for the attempt to establish New York was far more than the company officials favored spending. Although Matt was able to meet all expenses, business as well as personal, with his sales commissions in the past, now the expenses surpassed the sales. It was the investment Matt's parents had made that the company officials wished to tap to pay the mounting costs. They also offered Matt a territory in a questionable area in downstate Illinois if he was willing to sell his home and move his family there.

Neither Matt nor Carrie was agreeable to this arrangement. Matt was not fired, but he resigned.

Contrary to the wishes of the company's executives, Matt approached their competitor and went to work for him. In Michigan and neighboring states of Indiana and Ohio, he again piled up sales, which gave his former firm much competition. Matt and Carrie were determined to repay his parents. The investment made to Matt's former company had been held back, so they began repaying the loan with a monthly payment plan. After a number of months went by, Carrie hired a lawyer who finally was able to realize most of the money.

The last of Matt's deals involved a recording company. It was still the fifties, and tapes with music of various kinds had become the vogue. The recording company manufactured machines, which were sold in households, much as the cooking utensils had been. It was "hard-sell" again. This situation was to last for about a year. Then the parent company went bankrupt. Matt and his partner were left without time to diversify. Heartbroken, Matt, with Carrie's help, dissolved the business. They paid creditors, as they were able, negotiating for settlements that amounted to less than they originally were billed.

The irony was that now Matt enrolled in the community college, uncertain as to what he would do. NDEA funds were available, and Matt could qualify with only fifty per cent repayment if he was willing to teach in the inner city for five years.

Formerly, he recalled that in his sales position with the aluminum company, he had earned more than some of the teachers he had hired who had college degrees. They needed second jobs in order to meet the needs of their families. Now Matt was pursuing his education while they had become more established.

"We're going to have a lot less money now," Carrie reminded him.

"I don't care. I'll learn to live on what society is willing to pay me. At least I won't have to put up with the back-stabbing of the business world."

And so their lives entered into a new phase. Carrie had begun studies at the college while Matt traveled. Now it was she who changed jobs several times before finishing a two-year course at the college and signing a contract to teach an elementary class under the state's substitute-special arrangement. While she was teaching there for the second year, she learned of her pregnancy for this, her fourth child.

Chapter VIII
Timmy

I should have named you Samuel,
For 'ere the kiss of life had brushed your cheeks
You were promised, even as Hannah's son to serve.
The wisest tell me you may not.
For long I thought my promise made in vain
Yet He who gave you life showed me another path
Too wide for pride, too wide for vanity.

Carrie couldn't pinpoint the exact time when they noticed that
Timmy was having difficulties in learning. She did recall much later
that his first year ended with an ear infection causing draining from
both ears. Medicine had been prescribed and the doctor stated he
should be at rest. But Timmy wanted to run and play. He was large
at birth, weighing in at more than Matt had, leading his mother to
declare, "You have outdid yourself!" Speech came much slower

than for either of his older sisters, but he was able to make his wants known by sign language. From his high chair he would point at the mashed potatoes on the dinner table or whatever his taste buds desired. Carrie and Matt both chuckled at his pantomime of shaking the saltshaker.

When he did speak, his communication was loud. Besides that, his whole bodily movement was clumsy. He was what could be described as impetuous at his attempts to reach a destination or go after something. When Matt's job took him out of town, Carrie found that most of her time was spent caring for her son. She tried several preschools. In one, he lasted a month. Before his last day was completed, the director informed Carrie that Timmy had to mature somewhat more before being enrolled again. His transgression? He pulled one of the fish from the goldfish bowl and set it inside the bowl with the turtles. Somehow he should have known that turtles eat goldfish.

The second fared no better. This time the director informed her that while she felt sorry for Carrie, that she was carrying all the responsibility for her family while her husband was traveling, it was not working out well for her school. Timmy just did not fit in!

After waiting a month or two, Carrie attempted a third school. The hazard this time was a combination of skin rash from the sand pile and attempting to return home. Almost four now, Timmy ran away. Both times the police were called, for the director was frantic. How he had left the room where the children were lying down for rest time had never been explained. An elderly grandmother-type woman found him close to the railroad track a half-mile away from the school. He told her he wanted his mama. That was where Carrie found him after driving around in the vicinity of the school.

Each time Carrie approached Matt, expressing concern for Timmy, he answered with puzzling responses. "I don't see anything wrong. He's a boy, he's adventurous and different from the girls."

The girls? Sometimes it seemed there was a love-hate relationship between them and their brother, especially with Durinda. Was it because, having been the baby for four years before her brother was born, she had been given the attention that now seemed to focus mostly around Timmy? Giving the matter serious thought, Carrie decided to take a course of action to occupy Durinda away from the house. The downtown Y had classes for little girls ages seven to ten, with a variety of activities. One was the expression of imagination. Carrie vividly remembered how Durinda came home and told of a story she made up about the storm they had experienced the previous night. Also, she had formed a friendship with the bus driver, with whom she rode to the downtown Y each day. His route took him past their home and the stop for picking up passengers was at a corner less than a block away. Once, when Durinda was out playing, he drove past, and tooted his horn. When Carrie questioned her, Durinda replied, "Mom, that was *my* bus driver."

If Anna felt resentment toward Timmy, she did not manifest it as much as Durinda did. Yet she formed a protective manner for her younger sister. Always neat and tidy, she performed the tasks that Carrie had sometimes assigned to the younger girl. One day, when she came upon Anna folding the clothes for Durinda and placing them neatly in her sister's dresser drawer, Carrie questioned her, asking why she did not leave the chore for her sister.

"Mom, you don't understand her, she's different and likes to do different things," she defended. Different? Play-acting was one. She loved to dress up in old clothes and use Carrie's lipstick. Durinda could always be counted on to support Anna when her annual summer project took place. She planned a carnival, which involved most of the children in the block. They could dress up as clowns, princesses, or whatever imagination would lead them to choose. There were games and contests, lemonade and cookies, and other treats donated by the mothers in the neighborhood.

Once, when a summer shower interrupted their activities, Durinda walked across the backyard carrying the card table with games placed upon it on her head and shoulders, seeking refuge in the open garage. It was a comical sight, and a symbol of happy times in Carrie's memories.

Timmy had an assignment all his own. The willow tree that was planted in the farthest section of the backyard in the same year Timmy was born had grown enough for Timmy to use as the base for a tree house. The boy from early on was interested in building. By the time he was five, he began haunting the construction sites in the neighborhood. Within a radius of two blocks, former farmland that had been sold to a developer was now spawning a variety of ranch-style homes, popular in the fifties. Most children were advised the building sites were *off limits*. Not so with Timmy. He made himself endeared to the workers by handing them tools, sweeping up sections of scrapped wood shingles, and serving as a junior handyman. Carrie recalled the time she went to call her son for lunch and found him standing on a ladder with hammer in hand, pounding a nail. A worker was mentoring him, quietly showing him how to use the hammer. Later that same worker helped him collect the scraps needed for his tree house, loaded them in the trunk of his car, and delivered them to Timmy's yard at the end of his work day.

Timmy often arrived home after these episodical days with dust and soil on his clothes. When Carrie remarked surprise at the sight of his appearance, Timmy explained emphatically, "Mom, you know I'm a *builder*." He also began collecting tools. Sometimes he borrowed tools from the neighbors. That was ended when he failed to return them.

As diligent as Timmy proved to be with tools, school remained an enigma for him. If he knew the stories that Carrie and his sisters read to him, it was because he memorized them. The school and church relations brought painful thoughts and memories for Carrie. If she were ever to sympathize with Mary, the mother of Jesus, it was because she, too, as a mother, suffered to see her son struggle and experience rejection. Probably added to the rejections enacted toward her son was the hang-up of Carrie's memories of her own childhood rejections.

The year that Timmy was four, she finally was able to see him successfully complete nursery school at the Congregational Church. For his introduction, she had the good pediatrician to thank. He phoned both teachers, who were experienced and empathetic, and, most of all, determined to help Timmy. Large and strong, he was given the task of placing certain items in place. The boxes of building blocks, the toys and arrangement of chairs and tables, were all placed in designated areas with which Timmy was familiar. He learned about butterflies first-hand as one emerged from a cocoon. Songs, stories, and even attempts at dancing enriched his young life. Some compensation in contrast to the year before!

At that time Sunday school teachers and nursery attendants at the church were unable to cope with Timmy. He lacked the powers of speech to express himself, he was large for his age and appeared to be much older, yet was clumsy and a poor fit for the small quarters that allowed for the supervision of a group of youngsters. Added to this was the inevitable superstition and gossip that can occur when people take it upon themselves to pronounce a judgment about a situation that they do not understand. A former pediatrician had pronounced Timmy *retarded*. His criteria was that at the age of two, Timmy was unable to tell him that he was two. He had no understanding of developmental problems, nor did he pay much attention to the area of concern which Carrie attempted to bring to his attention: Timmy's hearing. At that time in medical history it was not the custom to help a child with fluid in his ears by inserting tubes to restore his hearing, help him develop his speech, and balance his frame.

When the Sunday school director came to visit Carrie and cite the problems with Timmy, asking her to exclude him from the nursery and Sunday school, Carrie became upset. Another rejection that she took to heart. Where were her friends? Who cared about Timmy, about her, about their family? To whom could she turn for help? What was to become of Timmy?

Desperate, she phoned another minister at a different church. She arranged to meet with him and after relating the problems she and Matt were experiencing in raising Timmy, he kindly offered to have Timmy enroll in their Sunday school. "We have a teacher with four little boys of her own. I'm certain she will be able to handle Timmy." And she did.

When the minister who had married Carrie and Matt missed their Sunday attendance, he came to visit, unexpectedly. Unlike their previous friendly relationship, he was now hurt and angry at their decision to change churches to accommodate Timmy's needs. He felt the problem stemmed from lack of discipline. "You don't spank him enough." He recalled Timmy patting a little girl at the church, while Carrie watched and did not reprimand him. Recalling the incident, Carrie was certain Timmy was only playing with her, attempting to be friendly.

The meeting left both the preacher and Carrie frustrated. Yet his final words to her proved later to be true. "You are running away instead of facing your problem. When you wear out your welcome at your new church, then where will you go?"

Painful words, these were. But the first minister was prophetic, for within a few years there was another parting, and advent to another church. This time it was a mission church, one that had an informal setting in a school gym. Here Timmy could be more relaxed, as were his parents. The only problem was that the school was about ten miles from home and required the family to travel a round trip of twenty miles each Sunday. Then, when Anna, and later, Durinda, entered studies for confirmation, it meant an additional twenty-mile round trip either on Saturday or a late afternoon in the middle of the week. They remained at the church for nine years, seeing it through its building program, growth and development, and the confirmation of not only the daughters, but eventually, Timmy.

Carrie went to see the minister at the second church. She could not understand how this man, who had welcomed their family so warmly just a few short years before, had become turncoat. The first minister had proven correct. It was not only the minister, but others were involved. It was the word of Timmy's kindergarten teacher that created hurt and anger in Carrie's heart. Although the kindergarten teacher was an RN and not a trained teacher, she took to heart her relationship with all the children, and particularly toward Timmy. How? She explained to Matt, "All I did with Timmy was speak softly to him close to his ear, and he always responded positively."

At the end of the year, however, it was decided that he should repeat kindergarten in order to grasp the materials more completely if he were to succeed in first grade. Church schools, it was believed, had a much higher standard than public schools for their students, and it was estimated that Timmy would not be able to compete. So Timmy joined the next class for another year. At this time, however, it was decided that he could not continue at the school and be enrolled in the first grade. *Why?* Carrie wondered.

Matt and Carrie approached the special education director at the public school. It was through the efforts of the church school principal that arrangements had been made for Timmy to be enrolled in what was considered to be the most desirable special ed class in the city. When the instructor came to visit at their home, she shook Timmy's hand. He wanted to give her a hug as he formerly had his kindergarten teacher, but she pushed him away, explaining to Carrie and Matt that she did not allow this type of personal touching with her students. She preferred to maintain her "professional stance." Observing Timmy further, she also commented on Timmy's size, stating "most of *these* children are bigger than average" and she would be working on developing their social skills. Eager to please her, Timmy brought her a picture he had made, for which she thanked him. How differently she responded to him from the way that his kindergarten teacher had.

What neither Carrie nor Matt could foresee were the problems that arose at this school setting. There were only about nine children in the class. Lessons were presented in a very slow manner. Timmy was trying. It was the lunch hour which caused difficulties. The school did not have a lunchroom or any supervision for the students at the noon hour. Many who lived close to the school went home. The special ed students, most of whom were bussed in from other parts of the city, were left on their own, for their teacher took her lunch hour away from the school. An aged parent at home required her attention. There was a sandwich shop about two blocks away from the school, and Matt and Carrie decided to arrange for Timmy to go there for his lunch, accompanied by some of his classmates. But there was no one to supervise the youngsters, other than the owner of the sandwich shop. Conflict arose among the young students. Two who were older and bigger in height and weight than Timmy, and who had been in the class the previous year, looked upon the newcomer as a rival. En route to the sandwich shop they became physical. Timmy, who could run, took off for Pop's and got in the door to avoid being beaten. Once inside the shop, the owner required order. Lunches eaten, the students returned to school. The older students again pursued Timmy. Once in class, they stopped, but Timmy did not. He retaliated. The teacher who had returned for the afternoon class observed this, and pegged Timmy to be the aggressor. Phone calls to Matt and Carrie resulted in Matt's decision to leave his own school during the lunch hour and drive to Timmy's, in order to accompany him during his own teacher's absence.

Matt's principal expressed concern that he, who sometimes was required to do playground duty during lunch hours at her school, needed to be excused to protect his son from the bullying he received from the older classmates. When the matter was brought to Carrie's attention, she approached his former kindergarten teacher, inquiring if Timmy had demonstrated this aggressiveness now reported by the special ed teacher.

"Never," was her reply. "Timmy always cooperated with me."

Then, conscience-stricken and concerned for her former pupil, she revealed to Carrie the problem behind the scenes at the church school. The problem lay with the first-grade teacher who had been the school's music teacher as well. She had taught hymns to the kindergartners and treated Timmy in a very strict and rigid manner. She shouted at him (and indeed, hearing was definitely a problem that no one had yet correctly diagnosed), which brought about a reaction. One time Carrie had observed the class during music time in Timmy's first year, and noted that he would crawl on all fours, emulating a puppy, which drew giggles from Timmy's classmates. In spite of Carrie's presence, the music/first grade teacher addressed Timmy, "My, aren't we the show-off today!"

When Carrie inquired of his kindergarten teacher if this happened in her class, she stated, "No, but some of the other children who are sympathetic to Timmy have asked me to tell the music teacher to be kinder to Timmy so he will not be a show-off."

The music and first grade teacher had no children of her own. Nor did she have any teacher training. Her field of interest other than music had been a training program of two years at a business college. She had had no child psychology or sociology, no education classes, and no previous teaching experience. She had been hired because she was willing to work for lower pay than an average public school teacher would expect. She and her husband had moved in from another state where they and their families had been members of the same denomination for several generations. Besides, she and her husband had become one of the major donors to the church's coffers.

It was Timmy's former kindergarten teacher who, prompted by Carrie's questioning and maternal concern, disclosed what had happened behind the scenes.

"It was the first grade teacher who didn't want him. She refused to have him in her class. The minister and the principal both begged her to reconsider, but she said *no*. And they're all afraid of her. Besides, she's greasing their palms. I told the principal that I believe Timmy is now ready for first grade. He answered, "Mrs. Holly, you just don't want to believe that you had him for two years and that he hasn't learned anything. They wouldn't listen to me."

When Carrie learned all this, she and Matt went to the administrator of the Special Ed program. They spoke of Timmy's situation, and asked that he be transferred into their district school's first grade. It was already six weeks into the school year, and she defended her own decision in placing Timmy where he was. She read to them the definition given her by the church school principal: "He cannot be contained in our school."

"I would certainly go back to these people and demand an explanation," she advised.

And so Matt did. "I had problems in the rural elementary school when I was a boy but they never excluded me from school."

When he confronted the minister, he retorted, "Can you contain him?"

That fall, however, the school had other problems. The principal of the former year had resigned to teach at a community college. His replacement was young and inexperienced. Anna, who was in his eighth grade class, was unhappy. Why? He was unable to carry out the discipline with certain youngsters that his predecessor had. She came home with sad classroom tales. So Matt decided when he and Carrie enrolled Timmy in the public school to transfer all three children into the same school in their district. Probably the one who missed her friends the most was Durinda. She did, however, make new friends very readily. Carrie arranged for her to have her close friend from the church school over for a visit as often as the mothers of the two young friends could work it out.

That fall, at the recommendation of the pediatrician and psychologists who had seen Timmy, Carrie and Matt decided to have Timmy seen by a pediatric neurologist and a specialist in hearing at Northwestern University in Chicago. Tests were conducted and the neurologist was certain that Timmy had far more potential than was evidenced. The psychologist also believed that his performance demonstrated a mind that was working very hard to grasp as much as he could learn. The speech and hearing clinic at Northwestern U ran other tests. The specialist there advised Carrie that Timmy would need tutoring help. The hearing loss that was evidenced was not great enough to place him in a deaf oral school, but they said he definitely needed added help.

Probably the most practical assessment of Timmy's situation was offered by the neurologist. "Mother, put on your blinders. This child is striving to reach his potential. Too bad his parents aren't a pair of share-croppers, instead of teachers. Place him back into the church school, for they have the most willing, helpful teachers for kids with special needs!" Yet his report was not respected by the public school system. Thus, Timmy was to remain in that class for the rest of the year.

Eager to have him succeed, Matt and Carrie hired a tutor who worked with him most of the year. He made some progress in reading. Spelling was difficult. Math, as well. The classroom teacher had no aide to help with children who needed special help. Timmy's tutor helped all he could and felt that with the added experience in summer school, Timmy could enter second grade. However, Carrie never did figure out whether it was actually a lack in Timmy's performance or egotism on the part of the public school teacher. When the tutor indicated that Timmy was reading at an acceptable level, she retorted, "But he doesn't get his arithmetic!"

The principal made the decision to exclude Timmy from school. He was now eight years old. Carrie had brought extra new math lessons home given to her by the first-grade teacher at her school. In fact, her school contained a special needs class for students like Timmy. Why had the city schools lacked these resources?

That summer both Durinda and Timmy were enrolled in a private Catholic school that offered reading classes. Both acquired higher reading levels. Yet Carrie and Matt had not been successful in re-enrolling Timmy in the public school, although he did need help with speech, for which he should have been qualified. He pronounced many words without prefixes. And as a result of his summer reading experience, he demonstrated his interests were expanded into other areas.

They were shopping for clothes when Timmy, browsing through the children's books, found one that described and included detailed photos of the human body. He picked up the book and approached Carrie. Momentarily she was out of his sight range, and when she located him after picking out a shirt his size, found him with tears in his eyes. He thought he had lost her. They bought the book, for she was happy to see his eagerness to learn via the printed word.

A different church school accepted Timmy's enrollment after much hesitation. But the principal stipulated a condition. "What about your other child, your daughter in junior high?" He implied that both children should be enrolled.

"Why don't you invite her?" Carrie suggested.

After a family consultation, it was agreed that Durinda would attend the church school with Timmy. When Matt was unable to drive them, they would ride the city bus. This meant double tuition as well as bus fare and lunch money, but Carrie and Matt agreed to shoulder the burden. Matt's parents offered to pay the tuition.

This lasted only for one semester for Timmy. It seemed that misfortune followed him, for the trained teacher who taught the special needs students became ill shortly after the fall session began. She was subsequently replaced by a series of substitutes, many of whom were not trained as well as the teacher assigned. With each sub there was a new adjustment. Lack of continuity lent itself to a lack of stability. In addition, Carrie realized, "We were outsiders. No one had to be accountable to us." By the time the semester ended, the principal decided that another change would be better for Timmy.

This change took place at the children's sheltered workshop at the very hospital where Matt's parents had once been employed. If the boy was at all puzzled by the many changes of schools he had attended, he was at least comfortable now. Academics were taught slowly so there was no pressure or frustration. Activities included a workshop where Timmy learned to work with wood. He made wooden toys and enjoyed the company of the instructor. Working with wood was to become Timmy's favorite activity, not merely as a subject, but as a pastime and occupation for the rest of his life.

"That's probably where you should have sent me in the first place," Timmy announced. It was at least safe from rejection, for most of the children required far more attention than Timmy.

Yet it was not Timmy alone who had changed schools. Durinda, who had changed with him, became attached to the church school. On the following year she was enrolled at the junior high that was located only a short walking distance from home. Newly opened, much was not yet organized to accommodate the enrollment attending the first year. Durinda lost a science book, stolen by someone whose family had not purchased one for him. Another student broke her glasses. He was described by Durinda's neighborhood friend as a smart aleck. Unlike the discipline enforced at the church school she attended the previous year, the merging of young people from different neighborhoods and social classes created disorder bordering on chaos. Teachers and administrators being immersed into a totally changing group dynamic were not yet oriented to the new environment. No one appeared to be accountable for a child's stolen book or broken eyeglasses. Thus, for a time, Durinda suffered lower grades. At one point she got in touch with a student from her former school and met him downtown to tell her woes.

If Durinda had approached either of her parents to discuss her frustrations, they would have acted on them. However, they seemed to be focusing on Timmy, assuming that since Durinda was not handicapped as was her brother, she would somehow overcome the obstacles the young teenager was meeting.

Probably the happiest incident that could occur for Durinda was the forthcoming new baby. She would take her mother by the arm and help her across icy spots in a protective manner. Durinda and Timmy would debate on the sex of their unborn sibling. Durinda wanted a baby sister. Timmy wanted a brother. His declaration was an open one: "We better get a boy. There's too many girls around here. If we get one more girl, I'm moving to Boonsboro!"

If there was rivalry between Timmy and Durinda, there was also a protective attitude between the siblings. Carrie recalled the time when Timmy took an extended walk away from home, and finding himself in unfamiliar territory about a mile away, he became frightened. Stopping at a gas station, he was helped by the attendant who sympathized when he saw the tears on the boy's cheeks. Fortunately, Timmy had memorized their home phone number. When Durinda answered, he cried, "Rindy, I'm lost, I'm lost!"

His sister's response was to ask the attendant for the location of her brother and then ride her bike directly to the spot where he waited. Happy to see her, he asked if he could ride on her bike, and learning the directions toward home, he drove off, leaving Durinda alone. Carrie drove the family car to fetch her kind daughter.

What would Timmy's future be? Carrie wondered. She pondered on the numerous rejections and changes in his life, changes which none of them seemed to be able to project or control. Frightened at the possibility that this new child might also be afflicted, she hoped for the little one to be like Anna, intelligent and artistic, verbally skilled and thoughtful of all those whom she loved, often going beyond expectations in showing charity and compassion.

But what of my dream for Timothy, when I was expecting him? she wondered. Her question was almost a prayer, a prayer which followed a promise she had made to the Almighty, that she was dedicating him to serve, if that would be the Lord's will for his life. Both his older sisters were verbally skilled, so why shouldn't he also have their talents? How could this ever happen? How much faith can he have in people after experiencing all of these rejections at such a young age? Will this interfere with his faith in God?

Chapter IX
The Saints in Carrie's Life

"How did you survive?" a friend asked Carrie when she learned that the death of Carrie's mother occurred when Carrie was only two years and four months old. In reply, she found herself repeating the answer she was given by a survivor of one of Hitler's concentration camps: "Good people." Now, as Carrie awaited the birth of her fourth child, she pondered the question again. How did she survive? Who were these *good people* who helped? What was it Tolstoy wrote about in his tale *What Men Live By?* Man can survive without parents but not without God. Carrie asked herself, was it God working in all of these people?

There was Grandma Fisher, who cared for the little girl during those months after Maria I was gone. Cheerful and loving, she never uttered a cross word. She always looked for the good in everyone.

In fifth grade there was Elizabeth Slutsky, who gave her the book, *Little Women,* and seemed to understand the child's need to know. It was she who was able to convince Anton that his daughter was ready for a challenge academically and persuaded him to allow her to skip the next semester of school. *Double promotion,* they called it. This procedure had been done during the previous year, but Maria II, influenced by a skeptical friend, had arranged for Carrie to be returned to her former class.

Then there were her godmother and godfather, Eve and Adam, who tried their best to be supportive. Whenever possible, they invited Carrie to visit them. Carrie always enjoyed the interaction with her cousins. Her older cousin, Lynn, was a strong influence on her younger cousin. The younger cousins, Lena and Ed, played games, sang songs around the piano, and enjoyed each other's company. Carrie experienced a sense of wholeness by their companionship, a sense totally lacking in the environment in her own immediate family.

Yet her most influential role model was Durinda Hansen. It was she who taught her to love Dickens and Shakespeare. It was she who showed compassion and caring, no matter what the situation happened to be. She told Carrie she was a pretty girl even when Carrie did not feel she was pretty. Always seeking a mother substitute, Carrie chose her teacher to be what she would like to become. Observing her mannerisms and orderliness, she decided this was what she would emulate. Even such details as an orderly purse with tidy compartments impressed Carrie.

Recollecting her early high school years, she found in reminiscing a deep appreciation for the compassion her high school teacher had demonstrated. It surely must have been a challenge at times. Childless herself, Durinda Hansen compensated for the void in her own life by mothering the girls in her homeroom. She also served as their English teacher. Carrie eagerly drank in every word of her expertise and reiterated much of the interpretation of the literature she studied in her class, a passion which earned her high grades.

Several times during her high school years, Durinda went to bat for Carrie. One time it was a personality conflict with the music teacher. Quite unlike Durinda Hansen, the music teacher threatened and scolded. Her classes were very large, her paper work was heavy, and unknown to Carrie until many years beyond her high school days, this same teacher went home to care for a sick mother after teaching all day. Perhaps between home duties and teaching duties, she had little time to rest and relax. The students felt the brunt of her difficulties. One day when she was remonstrating with the students, Carrie swore under her breath. The instructor, who heard her, reported it to Durinda. After confronting Carrie about her vulgar language, Durinda arranged for a meeting with the school counselor. Fortunately, he was aware of both sides of the situation. When he questioned Carrie, he asked if she was willing to repeat the inexcusable language, to which she replied, "No," and apologized. He then assigned her to a different music class in the "new" building. Carrie was happy because her cousin Lynn was enrolled in the same class. This change meant a different hour for music as well as a different hour for Spanish class.

The Spanish class was also in the "new" building and held a number of upper class persons. Here Carrie felt comfortable, for she loved to hear the Castilian accent of her instructor.

Geometry was difficult. For her successes, Carrie had Mr. Krebill to thank. He offered extra help to struggling students in preschool sessions, which Carrie attended faithfully. She managed to get acceptable passing grades as a result, but it was not until she became a homemaker, years later, that she found herself thanking him for the insights she gained in his classes. Her geometry experience, she believed, facilitated such tasks as moving a piece of furniture through a narrow doorway. Accuracy in hanging pictures, arranging flowers, balancing knick-knacks—all sorts of household maneuvers were accomplished more satisfactorily because of geometry. She was later to encourage her children to study the subject.

She wished she could thank many other saints, who helped her in various ways throughout her young life. Probably the two men who substituted for Anton were Uncle Jan, the husband of Maria III, and Pastor B. Years later, Maria III was to admit to Carrie that neither she nor her husband were adequately prepared for a teenager. Their young niece had just turned thirteen when they took her into their home. She was fond of their lifestyle and found a companion in her cousin at times, but Carrie also had a mind of her own. She attempted to weave in her desires with their customs and rules. Sometimes they clashed. Jan never struck her, no matter how trying the situation might be. He did let Carrie know when he disapproved of an action. Once he wrote her a note, pinned to her dress that she had forgotten to hang up in her closet.

"Karolina," it read, "you forgot to hang up your dress. If you're too tired to hang it up, next time tell me, and I'll hang it up for you."

Another time, Carrie rebelled against the strict measures imposed by Maria III. She had earned some money on a part-time job. Usually she turned over her entire salary to her aunt. From it, she would be given bus money and spending money. Unknown to her at that time, her aunt was banking the money for her. Carrie decided she would not continue to hand over her whole paycheck and just keep it for herself. Maria III was furious. On the following week, she worked full time, for it was now summer, and the mail order house needed her help. This time, to avoid more conflict, Carrie did hand the entire amount to Maria III in Uncle Jan's presence. His reaction was to take the envelope, pull out not only her bus fare for the week, but increase her allowance as a reward for presenting her entire pay. Years later, her uncle was to give these savings to her and Matt for a down payment on their first home.

The other father substitute was Pastor B. Carrie had many questions for him. He seemed to appreciate her interest in language. When she wrote a poem, he would sometimes help her by rewriting it. If she had a problem with her family, he listened and counseled. If she needed a change in attitude, he stated it candidly, but in a caring way. Most of all, she confronted him with theological questions. Some of her friends from school attended Moody Bible Church. Carrie wanted to join her friends. There were few in her own church. But she needed to resolve certain theological conflicts and questions. One was the question of infant versus adult baptism; another. the question of Holy Communion. Was it actually receiving the body of Christ, or was it merely representation? Pastor B. explained the Lutheran belief to her, the one in which she had been confirmed and had committed herself. The difference with the Moodyites, as he termed them, was that they regarded the rite of Holy Communion as an act conducted only in *memory* of the Lord's Supper.

"We believe we are receiving the body and blood of Jesus," he contrasted.

Probably the deepest question Carrie posed was that it was

difficult for her to understand the seriousness of Jesus' suffering and death.

"My dear girl, I have been studying theology most of my life, and I'm afraid that I also do not fully understand it," was his open response to her query.

Pastor B. always felt Carrie did not belong with Maria III and Jan. He hoped she would willingly return to her father's home. When she did return, because Jan took her there during her senior year in high school, he was happy. Perhaps his desire for her to return stemmed from the fact that she had never completely confided in Pastor B. She had never told him the entire story of why she had left. She ran away because she did not want to be beaten up any more. Maria II thought nothing about sparing the rod. Was Carrie afraid or too ashamed to tell him? Did he ever suspect the unstated facts?

Carrie recalled the tears in his eyes when he pronounced the confirmation blessing upon her, assigning the Scripture verse from Ephesians: *Be ye kind one to another, even as God for Christ's sake hath forgiven you.*

She did disclose the conflict she felt existed between Maria II and Maria III. He tried to reassure her that this would fade in time, although Carrie wondered if he truly believed this. Yet he stated it was *not* Carrie's problem. He advised her to leave it between them.

Another angel in her life? Sometimes she thought of Matt's mother in the early years of their acquaintance. More so, there was Matt's father, a kindly man who always upheld Carrie when she and Matt had disagreements. He graciously brought her flowers, planted daffodils and lilies of the valley in her yard, painted the house a pretty pink shade which Carrie selected, and complimented her for helping Matt with his sales work.

How about their grocer, Heinie? Carrie recalled their grocery shopping on the first Saturday evening after moving into their first home. They had walked three blocks to purchase some "vital vittles," as Matt termed them, and were just about ready to check out with two bags full when Matt, reaching for his wallet, discovered he had left it in the other trouser pocket, at home.

"That's okay. You can pay us on Monday. We're about to close right now, and we don't open the store on Sunday."

Overwhelmed by his trust, the young couple carried their groceries home, and Matt promptly paid Heinie when the store opened on Monday morning. There were other thoughtful favors. When Carrie needed special items, Heinie ordered them. When she was ill with one of her pregnancies, he delivered her groceries, sometimes personally.

There were other saints in the small business world: Gus, who delivered her dry cleaning; Chuck who filled all the prescriptions her family needed, and then waited patiently for payment, never dunning their family for past-due bills. One must not forget these people who struggle unobtrusively to run their place of business but do not lose the human touch.

Another father figure: Dr. Clarence, Carrie's English prof, who carried on where Durinda Hansen had left off in cultivating a deep love for literature in Carrie. "How richly blessed I have been," Carrie realized. She thought of an old Irish proverb: When one laments what is lost instead of taking stock of what one has received, mourning is an *unnecessary luxury*.

When Carrie enrolled in the church-supported college, she encountered serious believers among those who taught there. The one who always remained fresh in her mind was Doctor Marinus, the professor of education. He picked up on the enthusiasm Carrie demonstrated during her first year of teaching. His class met two afternoons weekly, at four o'clock, a time when Carrie, though exhausted from meeting the needs of thirty-five fourth graders, became rejuvenated just by hearing him speak. He moved away from the rigidity of tradition and encouraged her to meet diverse needs in her classroom. She expounded on these in her written assignments, recalling the care given her by certain teachers she had in her early years.

How about Dr. Rudolph, her first Russian professor at the fledgling college? Patient and thoughtful, he taught with dedication, believing, after his own life experience, that it was his duty to teach Russian. Having grown up in Moscow, though a member of the Latvian community, he was educated in the Russian language and was fully qualified to instruct students at the college level. A rather minor incident left a lasting impression on Carrie, right from the beginning of her attendance in his first class. It was a matter concerning the textbooks they were to use. Someone in the bookstore had made an error when placing the order. Instead of the beginning edition, only the second year text was available. Quietly, the professor addressed his class of sixteen students.

"Do not purchase this book. Through human error it has been made available instead of the book from which we will study. Until the proper textbooks arrive, I will have our lessons made up for you to use."

In the time of her greatest need, when Timmy was an infant and Carrie lay almost helpless in her bed, there was a cousin who offered timely help. After spending a day with her, she offered to take both Timmy, now six months old, and Durinda home with her, so Carrie could rest and recover without having to worry about the children while Matt was working. Etta, married to Matt's first cousin Josh, jokingly referred to herself and Carrie as "outlaws" who had married into the family. Of all of the three dozen first cousins, Etta remained one of Carrie's best friends from among Matt's family.

There were other saints that would enter Carrie's life that she would recount later. One in whom she often confided was *CC*, nicknamed because both her first and last name began with C. Carrie was never sure as to what were CC's religious beliefs, for she referred to herself as a *liberal*. Nevertheless, she was one of the best friends Carrie had. They were destined to have many adventures together. Though she did not spout religious phrases, it was she who never hesitated to stop and help a friend or lend a listening ear, an act which seemed to cut a troubled situation in half. She reminded Carrie of that old Russian proverb quoted by Solzhenitsyn: *The hands that help are holier than the lips that pray.*

Introspection brought about healing. Carrie came to realize the truth of Tolstoy's words, and came to understand that, contrary to her fears, she had never really been left *alone*.

Chapter X
The Crisis

When did her illness begin? Did it start only after Timmy's birth? Or was this a culmination of all that had preceded, throughout her twenty-five years, that brought about the crisis? And what part did the medication play in her illness? No metabolism test was administered throughout her pregnancy. Yet included with the vitamins in the pills given by her doctor's nurse, Carrie was informed, after the fact, were three grains of thyroid, to be taken daily. When she shared this information with a lab technician friend, she was informed this could have adverse side effects. And it surely must have, for later, when her rescuing physician ordered tests at the hospital, the radiologist informed her that the Geiger counter indicated an over-dosage. But he did assure her that her doctor would help her overcome the problem.

What Carrie did not know is that her obstetrician himself was in trouble. Within a year or so after Timmy's birth, he was indicted for drug addiction and sentenced to treatment at Lexington, Kentucky. His wife had died mysteriously. Rumors predicting the exhumation of her body for an autopsy abounded. The nurse who assisted him in his office became his wife six weeks after the death of his first wife.

It would be many years later that Carrie would recall how intimidated she had been by the seemingly pompous attitude the o.b. exercised towards her and his patients. Yet that did not seem to be the whole cause of her dilemma. Other matters entered in. Matt's contract with his aluminum company had been canceled, mostly because a former salesman approached him on joining with him for a larger income. Although Carrie looked upon this new arrangement as detrimental to Matt's employment future, he was persistent. "For my boy!" he declared.

Matt was indeed overjoyed at Timmy's birth. He affirmed his interest in his daughters, but the boy, he declared, "will get all my attention now." It seemed to be Matt's way of attempting to fill in the gap between himself and his own father. The elderly man had become almost a slave, in Matt's opinion, to the job he had at the hospital. Matt often recounted how, after his father's retirement, they had to hire several people to complete the work his father was required to do each day. His twelve-hour workdays went on for six weeks in succession; then he enjoyed a week off. There was little time and energy left for the attention his son had needed.

Timmy was two months old when they sold their first home. Now they prepared to move. Unlike previous postpartums, this was a cinch! All Carrie told herself she must do was to take those pills from the doctor. These would give her the energy she needed. Carrie was so happy at the birth of her son, as well as the new home they purchased, that she steeled herself away from the normal needs of a new mother and found herself overworked, too tired to think. They used all the savings they had to pay the down payment on their new home. Although it was not possible to furnish it in the manner that they wanted, they were happy to be settled in before Anna was to start first grade in her new school.

Somehow, the days fled by before she could accomplish all she had planned. One day little Durinda pushed her doll buggy down the sidewalk in front of their home. When Carrie went out the front door to check on her whereabouts, Durinda called out, "Mommy, won't you come and play with me?"

After offering a feeble excuse, a feeble explanation, she re-entered the house to continue her chores. Carrie did have a warning from an elderly friend who came to visit and noticed how clammy Carrie's hands felt. "You're not resting enough."

Timmy was not too easy to feed. He seemed to be hungry all the time. When he was six weeks old, Carrie stopped breastfeeding, and began feeding him cereal. Her Chicago visitor, a trained and experienced nurse, shook her head and declared after the infant cried half the night, perhaps from colic, "Too much solids, too soon. Why do they rush these babies so?"

That summer the Dutch cousins visited from the Netherlands with Matt's uncle and aunt. This uncle, older than Matt's father, was one of the nine brothers in their family. In addition, there were three sisters. Most had remained in Europe. Only two immigrated to the United States. Matt's other uncle lived in California. When his sister Beth traveled there, they opened their home to her and she resided with them for a time.

Although the visit with the Dutch cousins was welcome; it meant extra hosting for Carrie and Matt. Matt and his father, especially, were so happy to establish and renew these family ties, that in spite of her fatigue, Carrie was happy to expend the extra effort to entertain them and, indeed, it proved to be a long-term lifetime relationship for the cousins. There was much news to exchange: the war years, the German invasion, the peace and the subsequent Berlin Airlift which brought their mutual cousin, Harry, the son of Matt's uncle in California, to Europe. A pilot in the airlift, he was able to spend his leave visiting the family in Holland and become acquainted with them during his European assignment.

It was late fall when things began to close in on Carrie. One afternoon, after accompanying a neighbor whose son was close to Timmy's age on a walk with the little boys, she re-entered her kitchen through the garage door. Was it her imagination, or were the cabinets closing in on her? The grave mistake was that, after Timmy's birth, she had continued the pills administered to her during her pregnancy. Although this gave her energy to continue, it soon was evident that they could no longer hold up her strength. Then she began to skip meals. She was too tired to eat. By the first of November, she began to stay in bed most of the day. She managed to care for the baby, but finding him dissatisfied, added a bottle. Matt was forced to give up precious sales time so he could serve as chief cook and bottle washer, which he was not unwilling to do. One day, his mother came. She was very thorough, picking at the accumulation of cooking residue from the burners on the stove with a paring knife. The grating of the steel on the metal of the stove grated Carrie's nerves.

After days of this, Matt became weary and desperate. He lashed out at Carrie. "What's the matter with you? Even my mother can work circles around you!"

"But I can't sleep."

"You're not eating, either."

In desperation, they phoned the pastor of their church. He sat at her bedside trying to reassure her when she told him she felt that she was going to die.

"No, you're not going to die," and holding her hand he felt her pulse, adding, "your pulse is too strong."

That was when he suggested calling another doctor. He gave Matt his name and number to call.

Matt phoned and the doctor willingly made a house call on a fellow parishioner.

When Dr. Munson arrived early that evening, he brought his cheerful countenance into Carrie's room. Smiling, he greeted her, "What have we here?"

"I—I can't breathe!"

"No wonder. You're hyperventilating!"

"I can't help it," she replied in between the deep breaths.

"Yes, you can. Just hold your breath and count to twenty."

After making several attempts, Carrie found herself reverting to a normal breathing cycle.

"There, you can do it! Remember, just hold your breath and count to twenty if it happens again. Don't be afraid."

"I can't sleep either."

"We'll fix that, too. I'm going to give you some nerve tablets to help you sleep."

After leaving the medication at her bedside, and advising her to take just one tablet every six hours, he concluded his call, suggesting that she tell her o.b. he had been there.

For the first time in many nights, Carrie slept. Matt attended to the baby. Carrie could tell his patience and normal level of understanding had worn thin. Anna had eaten almost the entire box of chocolate-covered cherries he had brought home as a treat for Carrie, and he reacted harshly, perhaps reaching back to emulate the manner in which he may have been treated during his own childhood for such an action. Actually, she fibbed when first questioned. That may have been what set him off.

"You lied. I don't want my daughter to be a liar!" What a contrast to the attitude he had expressed after Durinda was born and Anna had pasted a sheet of postage stamps on some art paper. Then he had quieted Carrie's annoyance with "My little girl is more important than the loss of a few stamps!"

Now the concerns of earning a living and caring for a sick wife was taking its toll on the husband and father—the strong man who had always been carefree. As the week progressed, Carrie's situation did not improve, but seemed to reach a plateau. Carrie did call her primary doctor and described what had taken place. His reaction?

"Stop the nerve tablets because they will weaken you," he advised. "When can you come to my office?"

"I'm afraid someone will have to carry me in, I feel so weak," she replied, fearful she would be given another shot. The last shot seemed to throw her whole nervous system out of order. The "heebie-jeebies" she called them.

Her refusal to return to the first physician created tension between her and Matt. It was hard for her to explain her physical reactions, which ultimately came to light after Matt made new arrangements with Dr. Munson.

At Matt's request, Dr. Munson did return, and finding a lack of improvement in the young mother, he conferred with Matt, who questioned his plan of action.

"I won't call you cheap if you say no, but I believe she should be hospitalized. There we can observe more closely and run some tests to determine the true source of her problem."

Carrie found this hospital ward to be much different from

the maternity ward at the facility where her children were born. Nurses tried their best to be accommodating, but were bewildered by Carrie's condition. Prior to mealtime she was excruciatingly hungry, but when the meal was served, she couldn't eat. It seemed that someone had closed the entrance to her stomach, tightened it, and made it impossible for her to consume the food set before her. Her roommate tried to advise her when the shaking began. Her hands appeared red, and she appealed to the nurse who brought her meal, "Look at my hands!"

The physicist who had used a Geiger counter gave one of the first tests ordered by Dr. Munson. Carrie questioned him, asking about the count of roentgens.

"I see you've been reading." He assured her the test involved no more than that in a normal t.b. X-ray, and after listening to the Geiger counter, he confirmed that her thyroid count was indeed high, but assured her it could be treated, and that he would report the results to the doctor immediately.

Returning to her hospital room, she found that the challenges had returned. She was able to read while lying down, but when rising from the bed and attempting to walk around, she lost all mental focus. There were a few glimpses of normality. She visited the two young women in the room next to hers. Their music was soothing. They introduced her to Elvis Presley and *Love me tender*, and *Can't help falling in love with you*. Chatting with them, Carrie realized how much her complete attention to the new son and her family had isolated her from what was happening to others, to the rest of the world, though she did recall the news announced about the death of Babe Dedrickson Zaharias, who had been her high school heroine.

Between these short respites she experienced sheer torture. Carrie tried to come to grips with herself. Her roommate had had three-fourths of her stomach removed. When her husband visited her, he was delighted to learn that for the first time in years she was able to enjoy a cup of coffee. She tried to advise Carrie not to read the favorite psychology book she had brought with her. Later, when Dr. M. stopped, she made it a point to tell him her diagnosis. "Doctor, she reads that crazy book and then she acts crazy."

His response surprised Carrie. "Listen, lady, what my patient does is strictly between her and me."

Carrie, feeling guilty, pointed to the door, indicating she wanted to talk with her doctor privately. He nodded, and helping her out of the bed, allowing a minute for robe and slippers, he accompanied her into the hallway where she pleaded with him to change her room. "That woman just had three-fourths of her stomach removed, and I do not want to add to her troubles or hurt her more in any way. I can't help what is happening to me, and when it does, she becomes distressed."

"Exactly what is happening, Carrie?"

She told him about wanting to sleep in the daytime, about her wakefulness at night, and the contradictory signals she received from her stomach, the "heebie-jeebies" as she termed them. Puzzled by her condition, but determined to help and get to the bottom of her situation with an accurate diagnosis, he paused to consider the tests already completed. Her blood pressure was at high normal. There was temporary diabetes. The physicist had already reported the hyperthyroid condition, as he had promised Carrie.

"I can give you something to help you sleep, and regulate your day. As for your roommate, if she had three-fourths of her stomach removed, she has had problems for a long time, long before she ever met you. In no way are you to blame for her situation. But I think I will run one more test tomorrow: a blood chemistry test. Carrie, I have frequently seen these post-partum disorders which you are now experiencing."

Exactly what the results were, Carrie was never certain, but a change in medication was administered, and now the doctor began talking of sending her home. Beside her bed she had propped up the photo taken of all three children together—Anna and Durinda hovering over Timmy, and all three dressed in red polka dot on white night clothes. How she loved those children, and wanted to be well for them, and overcome the fears she had of leaving them, as her diseased mother had left her.

****

Her reminiscing was interrupted by another shot of oxytocin. This had to work, and the little one had to be born healthy. "Please God," she pleaded. Not a repetition of the difficulties Timmy had.

How different things were now, in this hospital, where the older children were born. She recalled Timmy's birth. It had happened so fast. She had only been registered a short time, and the pains were not severe. Nurses and a resident waiting outside the labor room door were asked about their gathering. Someone replied they were waiting for "the big splash," and within forty-five minutes, her son was born. When she questioned the o.b. who delivered him to identify the gender, he replied, "Hear that cry? You've never heard a cry like that in your house before."

She recalled saying she really wouldn't mind another little daughter, but feared her husband would be disappointed, because he wanted a son. Indeed, Matt was happy. Matt was always excited about each new child, and was looking forward to this one as well.

****

When Carrie experienced another repetition of hunger pains, and then hunger loss, she began to cry. "I must be losing my mind," she told Dr. Munson.

"No, listen to me, Carrie. You are *not* losing your mind."

When he announced that she would be dismissed from the hospital on the following day, a week after her admittance, she expressed fearfulness.

"I don't want to hear talk like that, or we're all through, right now!"

Arranging for an appointment in his office within the following third day, he assured her that he wanted to help her and to help her family.

When Matt brought her home, dinner was ready. Unlike previous evenings, Durinda had picked up her toys and placed them in the toy box. Later, the four-year-old hung up her clothes and washed and brushed her teeth. Matt had established a routine for the children to follow during their mother's absence. Two neighbors had volunteered to stay while Matt made his nightly business calls. He admitted his sales were at an all-time low, but he assured her, "We'll manage."

How did they manage? she asked herself now. They borrowed funds to make the payments on the new home, utility bills, and groceries. It meant a mortgage on their household goods with rather steep interest payments, since all of their savings had been depleted.

Carrie dressed carefully for the office appointment with Dr. Munson. She even wore earrings, something she had not done for months. Matt had taken her to Irina's to have her hair done. "My, how long your hair is!" her hairdresser exclaimed. "Let's trim it a bit, to shape it." Irina was one of the real friends, and a saint in Carrie's life.

When Carrie met with the doctor, he was indeed pleased with her appearance and, even more so, with her attitude.

"How wonderful you look!"

He spent some time in conversation with Carrie, who related some of her family history, her early motherless childhood, her goals to acquire an education *someday,* her marriage and her family. Then, before leaving with an appointment again for the following week, along with a new prescription, he repeated his pleasure at seeing Carrie looking so well, and he spoke assuredly.

"If you can come this far in just three days, you're going to be fine!"

Actually, it would be a matter of months, perhaps six, before Carrie again felt like a whole person with energy to be the wife and mother she wanted to be.

Aunt Anna, the sister of Matt's mother, came to help her for a day. She reported Carrie's situation to Etta, who followed her, with help.

The wife of Matt's cousin, her best friend in his family, came for a day to help and took both Timmy and Durinda home with her. For in spite of the doctor's positive prediction, Carrie found she tired easily, and on the day of Etta's coming, she spent much of the time in bed.

"You need to rest up, and I don't have anything preventing me from taking care of your two younger ones while you recover," she assured Carrie.

Christmas was lean. There were a few toys for the children and some much needed clothes. Carrie wore her old knit dress, the style of the fifties, on Christmas Eve. What mattered most to her was that she and Matt could attend the church service. The organ prelude played "Lo, how a rose 'ere blooming" that remained a permanent memory. Friends greeted her. One advised, "You got to learn how to relax, kid," and another who had sent a reassuring card with words written, "Our thoughts and prayers are with you," greeted her warmly.

January found Matt applying for a new job. Former colleagues who had been in the aluminum ware sales had tried to recruit Matt to join them, but Carrie was not in favor. With family responsibilities as they were, the couple agreed Matt now needed a job with regular hours and regular pay. One attempt after another came to a dead end. Then a friend who was leaving his firm called Matt to tell him of the position that would be open as his replacement. He introduced Matt to his employer, who was eager to contract Matt. And so it was that Matt became a traveling representative for a food company. His contacts took him all over western Michigan. He met with cooks, food purchasers, and school superintendents, as well as other administrators and employees who were in charge of ordering and preparing meals for their institutions.

Although this job was invigorating for Matt, he disliked nights away from home. Some contacts periodically took him into the Upper Peninsula. Then it was neither practical nor possible for him to drive home because of forbidding distances and the need for multiple contacts in a particular area. He often stated that he missed not having Carrie with him to share the scenery and experiences he encountered in his travels.

The enhanced income proved welcome, but there were new challenges dealing with the corporate world. Matt was much too naïve and trusting to realize these ambiguities until they caught him in a difficult situation. Conflict of interests brought about by envy among certain executives forced him to resign his position the following year. He entered into another position with a competitor and developed his own clientele. After two years he re-entered direct sales with a company that manufactured tape recorders and equipment. Again, with the help of an aide, he developed a sales organization, but within a year the manufacturer went bankrupt. Unable to diversify rapidly enough to save his business, Matt was forced to dissolve it. He avoided bankruptcy himself by paying as many creditors as possible, negotiating partial payment as settlement after explaining his situation.

It was at this point that Matt changed the course of his life completely. With Carrie's encouragement, he enrolled in college. Prior to this time, Carrie had taken the advice of Dr. Munson to enroll in evening classes at the local community college. Timmy was now three, and the girls were seven and nine. She had a reliable babysitter for the evenings. There were many questions Carrie sought to answer on the meaning of life, and she began part-time college studies, hoping to search in earnest. But her goals were now interrupted in order for her to focus on helping Matt pick up the pieces of his life and continue on his new venture.

Matt's goal was to take courses and see where they led. At first he thought he wanted to enter the ministry, but in the end he decided to teach. Unlike his previous thoughts, centered on entrepreneurship, on making money, he would accept, he said, what society was willing to pay him for his services. And so, the new venture in his life began.

Chapter XI
The Search

When did it begin, Carrie's intense desire to know, to become content with convincing answers? It probably all began after Timmy was born, after her illness, which took place when Timmy was six months old. It was a private quest, one she could not even share with Matt. True, there was the medication, the injection of hormones, which threw her physical self into confusion. She asked Dr. Munson, "What part of this is mental and what part is physical, it's so hard to tell."

"That's something you will have to figure out, but I'm sure you will as time goes by." His answer led her to wonder.

At the hospital she had tried to read her Bible: *Romans*, Paul's letter, wherein he spoke of the renewing of one's mind. How could she renew her mind? She felt herself caught up in a vise. Yet, she wondered, was this of her own making? Thoughts reverted to her childhood. When people at her church talked about God, Carrie wondered where He was. Was He really there, when the worship service was taking place, as her Sunday school teacher declared?

Engraved in her memory was the end of the worship service at the church of her childhood, when the Benediction was chanted. She remembered how her Sunday school teacher, who sat in the front pew with her parents, would bow her head three times. With each *Hospodin* the tall feather on her hat was lowered, in perfect rhythm with the three parts of the Aaronic blessing: *The Lord bless thee and keep thee, the Lord make His face to shine upon thee, the Lord lift up His countenance upon thee and grant thee His peace.* The young girl discerned the reverence implied in these physical motions, and became convinced that what her teacher had been teaching was what she sincerely believed.

How could she ever describe the soul-lifting feelings she experienced as she watched the choir entering each Sunday singing *Krasny Jezhishi*—Beautiful Savior? The chanting of the words of institution preceding Holy Communion? Or the words of Isaiah 6, when sung by the choir as the first communicants approached the altar to receive the sacrament? Or all music, the drama and ritual? Years later, when she studied Russian history, Carrie understood what the emissaries Vladimir had sent to Constantinople, where they attended worship in Saint Sophia's Cathedral, had experienced. They reported to their leader, "It was as if we had been in heaven, itself."

If her soul was lifted to unreachable heights, the experience was temporary. The service ending, Carrie returned to the everyday realities her life offered. She endured some teasing from classmates, the verbal abuse from Maria II, and the vulnerabilities resulting from a lack of one-to-one guidance that only a mother or worthy mother-substitute can offer a growing child. She performed her chores gladly, completed her lessons, and tried to please her stepmother. She wanted only approval, and something approaching assurance that she was loved. Anton's absence in the evenings, and the cares of being the breadwinner left little opportunity for either Carrie or her sisters to receive the paternal attention they needed. The younger girls fantasized with the cutout dolls. What Carrie fantasized were half-adult dreams in a child's mind, influenced by the romance magazines she secretly read that were given to Maria II.

Religion as it was taught assumed somewhat of a regimented activity. One recited prayers at bedtime: the Lord's Prayer; the Ten

Commandments; the Apostles' Creed. Catechism was learned by rote and Scripture verses were memorized. An automatic religion. Yet Carrie saw very little of what she had been taught applied into action. There were family disagreements. Some cursing took place. Carrie recalled how she repeated words she heard uttered by her father's younger brother in her second-grade classroom. Shocked by the little girl's language, her teacher sent for her parent. What happened after that, Carrie could not remember. Was she punished for imitating her uncle's vulgarities? Even old Anna, the matriarch, who had not mastered the English language, used foul language at her alcoholic son. When cautioned that children were listening, she unrealistically retorted that they were not supposed to be listening.

It wasn't that old Anna was an unbeliever. Rather, in certain situations, religious teachings were not integrated into everyday life. Anger produced regression.

Was it habit or custom that led Carrie to seek out a Lutheran church in Matt's hometown? Their culture, understandably, differed. Unlike her childhood church, members here were second generation or earlier, born in America. The same serious momentum of her childhood church did not appear here. No matter that the minister and all were kind to her, Carrie could not shake off the feeling that she was an outsider.

Ultimately, she began to look back, trying to find some beginning.

When she began to recover, Carrie wrote to Anton. She told him of her illness. He had already been informed of it by Matt's mother, who also told him in a letter of her sister's visit and help from both her sister and sister's daughter-in-law, who was married to Matt's cousin. His reply was that they would all be blessed for helping his daughter. After spending a day with Carrie, and seeing how limited she was, remaining close to her bed, Etta, Matt's cousin's wife, offered to care for the two younger children for the following week in order to allow Carrie time to rest and recover.

Included in Anton's reply to Carrie was information about the family of Maria I. No one had ever told this to Carrie before. Maria I was the oldest of four sisters and the only one who came to America. Her father had been a veterinarian, specializing in the care of horses prior to World War I. He was forced to serve in the military of Austria-Hungary, as were many Slovak men. Returning home wounded, he died of a kidney ailment, but not before he was to father a son, the youngest of his children.

Seeing the financial struggles of her mother and family, Maria I decided to go to America. Her mother's younger brother, Michael Fisher, expressed a willingness to sponsor her. Maria I, who was already experienced at caring for younger children, was able to be employed as a nanny in the homes of some of Chicago's wealthy families for several years.

It was at the Slovak church that she met Anton. Quiet, shy, Anton must have been enchanted with this outgoing energetic young maiden who shared the common history of their native land. But why did they leave it? They loved the language. They loved the customs. They loved the food. Always there was hospitality, especially on holidays and special events such as birthdays, anniversaries, weddings, and even at funerals.

Was it in English I or English II at the community college where Carrie was eventually enrolled that her real search began? The search was for more history, more understanding of her parents' people, a search for meaning in her own life, and a search for how she was supposed to relate to God.

Causal analysis. Comparison and contrast. The first English prof may have been somewhat provocative, but he had stimulated her thoughts. These led her to the threshold of understanding herself as a person, possibly even more than any psychiatrist might have. Besides, what did her doctor report to Matt about that possibility during Carrie's illness?

"I'd introduce her to a psychiatrist, but I don't know any who would get along with her."

Why? Carrie wondered. "What's wrong with me?"

Trust? Whom can one trust, really trust? So many people whom Matt had trusted and whom she wanted to trust, had let them down. His supervisors of the aluminum company. The doctor who delivered Timmy, as well as their two daughters. He himself wound up in Lexington, Kentucky, for drug rehab about a year or so later.

Outside reading was required. Ah, here was a tie. *Dr. Zhivago* wherein one word caught her eye and reached down into her language experience from childhood: *strelnikov*, the hunter, the Slovak hero resembling the British Robin Hood was a *strelnik*. He was forced into it by the monstrous retaliation of his father who absented himself from his serfdom duty because of his wife's illness and death. When *Janošik* learned of the brutality, he became an outlaw who championed the cause of the oppressed people until he was caught and executed. Never before had Carrie realized the close language ties between the Russian and that of her father's native language.

This was the Cold War. Russian imperialism, by agreement at Yalta, had placed her mother's family behind what Churchill called *The Iron Curtain.* Carrie was to learn there are actually a variety of Slavic languages. They all seemed to stem from the ancient Macedonian. Yet the Cold War with its publicity had led many Americans to believe that all Russians were enemies. Communists were bad. McCarthy continued to threaten his colleagues in the Senate as well as the administration, continuously declaring how evil they were. And what of her mother's family? Carrie had two aunts and many cousins behind the Iron Curtain. If there were to be a war, did this mean that they would have to shoot at her children, or that her children would have to shoot them? She recalled the true account given by the late pastor's wife of her brother coming upon a Slovak soldier during his mission as a sniper during World War I. Sensing the American, whose duty it was to annihilate him, the soldier who had been forced to fight for Austria-Hungary, knelt in prayer: *Otče naš* ... Hearing the familiar words of the Lord's Prayer, he himself learned in childhood, her brother could not bring himself to shoot this man, with whom he shared a common tongue and a common faith. Instead, he spoke with him a few words in the language that both found familiar. "Go in peace," he urged him, "and tell no one what has happened between us." But the Americanized Slovak returned home from World War I and he did share this experience with his family and friends.

Were the Russians all bad? Carrie wondered about this until she began her studies in the language at the fledgling college near Grand Rapids. It was during her second year of study with the Swiss professor that she received a more objective view. When Yuri Yevgenin flew into space, the Russians had a triumph over the United States. Professor T., as the students referred to him, thought this was a marvelous victory for the Russians, one that Americans should applaud.

"You have everything here. Consumer goods, comfortable homes, cars, beautiful books, a standard of living far above that of the Soviet people. Now they have something to be proud of."

Yet, Carrie considered, if their schools are better than ours, why? She looked back upon her research into the life of Masaryk, while studying English II. Had his dream for Czechoslovakia been dashed? This nation he helped to create from the ashes of old Austria-Hungary had hardly begun to fulfill its destiny before it again suffered under German rule. Now this country was under the mantle of the Soviet Union.

While reading and preparing her report for English II, Masaryk and his thoughts as expounded upon in Karel Čapek's book became important to Carrie. Here was a man whose father had lived in a state of serfdom, but he became educated and rose above his father's station and ultimately served to lead his people to nationhood. What were his ideals, his politics? Plainly stated, *Jesusdom*. What a removal from the emotional and rigid traditional formality to which Carrie had been introduced during childhood and her teen years. When he spoke of Jesusdom, Masaryk literally desired to follow the teachings of Christ and use them as the bulwark philosophy to develop and guide his nation.

What was it Christ did? He healed the sick, fed the hungry, warned the rich, showed loving care for children, taught the thesis of the kingdom—not only to His disciples, but all who followed Him and heard His words of comfort and hope. This was the foundation Masaryk wished to use to build his state. Not totalitarianism, but Christian socialism. A government that sought to care for its people, to educate, nurture, and provide in such a manner that individuals can become responsible and independent, yet caring human beings.

What of the divine nature of Christ taught by priests and pastors, theologians? It was not they who had convinced Carrie. When she began to read Masaryk's words, Carrie knew that, finally, she had found someone whose faith she could emulate. Masaryk termed Christianity as *revelation par excellence*. Why? It was the fact that God took on man's flesh and dwelt among men for many years. Jesus taught and lived the example of His teachings for His entire life on earth. These were the teachings upon which Masaryk formed his political philosophy, and on which he based his political ideals, to pursue the *just cause of Christian Socialism.*

There was much about Masaryk's leadership that Carrie admired: his statesmanship; his continued hope for his people in spite of centuries of hardship; the welding together of the Czech prisoners of war after persuading their Russian captors to release them to defend the freedom of their own people at the closing days of World War I. And finally, the fact that a grateful infant nation bestowed the honor of the first presidency upon him.

There was something else that stands as a historical fact. It is this leader's willingness to fearlessly stand for truth in spite of possible unpopularity, such as the time he defended the Jewish citizen accused of ritual murder. As the champion of the accused, Masaryk became the spokesman not only for the people of Czechoslovakia, but even for the world at a critical time in history.

As admirable as all of these qualities were, it was not the heroics he exemplified that persuaded Carrie. It was his faith, openly declared and undoubtedly the basis for his action. Neither money nor power influenced or cajoled him. What was this basis? Carrie had heard the words he stated many times before, but, now, they formed a culmination of her search:

"Seek ye first the kingdom of God and His righteousness, and all other things shall be added unto you."

It was as if she had finally come home, had stepped on the threshold of that which she had been searching for most of her life. Here it was, not from the mouth of a clergyman, but from the words of her father's kinsman. Faith had new meaning for her and a goal for the fulfillment of her life. Now she was prepared for whatever the future held for her, for her and Matt, for her and her children, no matter what challenges they would face with and for Timmy, and for this new child they awaited to be born. For the first time in her life, she had words she could sink her teeth into, so to speak, a belief that this man, her father's countryman, could offer as real, meaningful, an ideal she could follow, forever and ever, without fear. Amen.

Chapter XII
The Fullness of Time

The day had been a long one. Now it was evening. Already more than twenty-four hours had passed since the police sergeant had ordered the police ambulance driver to take Carrie to the hospital. Yet it seemed as if it had been an eternity away. All day the pains started and then stopped. *Were the shots helping at all?* Carrie wondered. Just so they don't hurt the baby. Timmy, the nine-year-old, had endured enough, and she and Matt had suffered along with Timmy. If one wants to hurt a person, hurt his child!

Neither Carrie nor Matt cared which gender this baby might be. They just wanted a healthy child. Of course, their children expressed differing preferences. Durinda wanted a girl, a little sister. Carrie remembered how protective her second daughter had been during the early months when she first learned of her mother's pregnancy. During the winter months she took her mom's arm and guided her on the icy walks. She expressed true happiness about their forthcoming baby.

As for Timmy, he wanted a brother. "Too many girls around here. We need another boy. If we get another girl, I'm moving to Boonsboro!"

Anna did not express a preference. She just wanted to be helpful to her mother and tried her best to relieve her from heavy chores in their home. The whole season had been a busy one for Carrie. Advanced as her pregnancy was, she continued her studies until the middle of June. She was enrolled in three courses at the college in town. Then, on three afternoons weekly, she drove fifteen miles to attend the Russian classes at the fledgling college west of the town. No seat belts were yet required. They were still considered a novelty for travelers.

Carrie wondered, *if I did have an accident, wouldn't a seat belt crush the baby?* Anyway, she was exhausted during the final exam, declaring when finished writing, "Now I'm going home to wait for my new baby!"

One course in English Lit, which she loved, proved to be almost too much. Eager to teach all he could, the professor gave numerous handouts to enrich his students. Finally, Carrie was reduced to merely skimming the papers. She had to give somewhere. She recalled how one Saturday afternoon, when she should have been studying for the forthcoming test on Monday, she spent her time reviewing the baby clothes she had packed away. One by one, she sorted through the garments, nighties, panties, boys' clothes from Timmy, a few precious girls' things from Durinda and Anna. It seemed her soul was divided between her family and her book-loving mind. She recalled having read during her Psychology course about a woman who wanted to write, but felt stifled until she married and had a family of her own to fill in the gap she had experienced in a dysfunctional home during her childhood. Now, attaining a sense of wholeness, she found herself able to release the dormant expression buried deep within her soul since early childhood.

The sixth shot of oxytocin. Aha, finally. Labor had become intense. From five minutes apart, to only two, and then one minute between pains. Carrie was taken to the delivery room where she recalled the deep-breathing exercises for which she had been prepared in prenatal classes.

"That's fine, just keep it up, now push," the doctor directed. Matt was there beside her. Unlike the restrictions husbands had when Anna was born, they were not just allowed, but welcomed into the delivery room to give support and encouragement to their wives.

It was almost sixteen years since their marriage. So many good times. So many mistakes. So many challenges. Some conflicts. Yet the most endearing traits Carrie found in Matt were his closeness to the children and willingness to care for the needs of his family. There had been this restlessness which she confided to Dr. M.

"What can I do about his restlessness?" she asked, hoping for advice.

"Nothing. Just give him a happy home life."

Yet Dr. M. expressed impatience with Matt, especially when his nurse reminded him of the increased overdue bill. "Please don't bother me about the bill," he replied. "There's nothing I can do about it right now."

The truth of the matter was that Matt had his hands full trying both to help at home and interview for a job to take care of the finances. No longer satisfied with a factory blue collar job, he set about interviewing for sales positions advertised by large companies. They wanted someone with a college education. Matt had never needed a college education to sell aluminum cookware and had, in fact, fared better than most of his contemporaries who had sheepskins. There were changes in jobs with a keen interest in succeeding, yet ambition without reason. Once, he took a psychological profile test when applying for a sales position; he was told that his personal aggressiveness was not balanced with a practical judgment. The company was willing to hire him, but the cause was lost when they assigned his training to an insecure, incompetent, newly-hired executive who looked upon Matt as a rival. The trainer was particularly annoyed when he learned of Matt's visit with the company's executive at the country club.

"Wow, they treated you better than they treated me," he complained. Matt returned to aluminum cookware sales, his employment "home" for several years. Boredom from repetition, yet something he knew he could handle. But what was he seeking? It was this that eventually led him back to school with the mental stimulant he longed for and had not realized until he had tried other avenues of endeavor. It was this summer, while awaiting the arrival of his fourth child, that Matt would conclude the studies leading to his B.A. degree in special education as well as elementary education. It would not be until years later that he wished he had pursued teaching at higher-grade levels, perhaps high school or college. He loved geography and enjoyed teaching social studies. The mundane courses such as spelling, elementary math, reading, proved to be repetitive and boring. In addition, the elementary field was a woman's world. Matt found himself alone, except for the male custodian. Even the small restroom beside the office was unisex. What made the situation tolerable and interesting was dealing with the personalities of the students and their families, products of the inner city. It was this part of his teaching task that had been helped by his sales experience and the inter-personal action with people who were interested in his products.

We're tardy with life's pursuits for us, with our education, fulfilling satisfying goals, but why? Carrie wondered.

It was just as she had declared to Matt earlier, a *tardiness in nature.* True, on both their parts. We did things kind of backwards. Married. Had children. Bought a home, and then another home. Assumed responsibilities that required more maturity than we had at the beginning. Why? What was it told to Lear? The words of Shakespeare haunted Carrie. We became older before we became wise. There was so much to overcome. Corporate finagling. Matt trying to find his niche. Carrie wanting both a family and a career.

The pain was intense.

"Push, now," directed Dr. Prompt. "You can do it. Your breathing is deep. Excellent."

Carrie was thankful for the prenatal lessons. She had never been this well prepared for the birth of her other children. Yet for this one, she had waited twenty-seven hours.

Then she heard the cry. It was over. Or had it just begun? This new life.

"What, what is it?"

"Just what you wanted. A beautiful baby."

Carrie did not press the doctor further. Instead, as she watched Matt pull out a cigar from his shirt pocket and hand it to the doctor, she gazed at the child, touched by the wonder of all that had transpired before this new little one entered the world, and she uttered, "Thank You, God. Thank You."

Made in the USA
Middletown, DE
01 February 2020